D0384498

BATTLE MOUNTAIN

Little, Brown and Company

Hachette Book Group
237 Park Avenue, New York, NY 10017
Visit our website at www.lb-kids.com

Little, Brown and Company is a division of Hachette Book Group, Inc. The Little, Brown name and logo are trademarks of Hachette Book Group, Inc.

The publisher is not responsible for websites (or their content) that are not owned by the publisher.

First Edition: October 2012

ISBN 978-0-316-18874-6

10 9 8 7 6 5 4 3 2 1

RRD-C

Printed in the United States of America

BATTLE MOUNTAIN

BY RYDER WINDHAM
WITH JASON FRY

Ⓛ Ⓑ
LITTLE, BROWN AND COMPANY
New York   Boston

CONTENTS

Chapter One
JUNKYARD AMBUSH!

Standing in a huge junkyard in the Nevada desert, surrounded by piles of wrecked cars and trucks, Ironhide knew a fight was coming. He just didn't know when.

A living robot with bright blue optical receptors and black-and-silver metal plating, Ironhide was from the planet Cybertron. He was also a friend and follower of Optimus Prime, the leader of the Cybertronian faction known as the Autobots. Because Ironhide's sensors included night-vision optics, he could see everything in the darkness clearly. As he surveyed the ruined machinery and twisted scraps of metal all around him, the hulking Autobot didn't bother trying to determine which vehicles had been used until they were damaged beyond repair and which had wound up in the junkyard because of human neglect. He was just glad that none of the ruined machines had ever been alive, because then the forlorn resting place would have been a real graveyard.

Still, he thought, *it sure* looks *like a graveyard.*

Ironhide didn't believe in ghosts, and very few things in the universe scared him. But he didn't like the idea of fighting in an area filled with so much battered and forgotten scrap metal. The sight brought back too many harsh memories—memories that he didn't like to think about.

The scarred old Autobot shook his broad head. *Enough stinkin' thinkin'. There's work to be done.*

He took a cautious step forward. He had oiled his joints so he could move quietly, but it was impossible to make himself entirely noiseless. He looked around. Although it wasn't uncommon for rats and other vermin to live in junkyards, Ironhide was not surprised that he didn't see any. He was certain that he was the only living thing within the confines of the junkyard's rusty metal fences.

But he was also certain he was not alone. He knew he was being hunted.

Ironhide took another step forward. The impact of his giant metal foot on the ground caused a nearby pile of bent and twisted car doors to bounce slightly. Out of casual routine, he performed a quick check of the primary weapons built into his metal body. His arm cannons, missile launchers, and megabazooka were all operational. Satisfied with his weapons status, he then checked his other systems. His optical, auditory, and olfactory sensors were all operating normally. They didn't detect any traces of another entity in the junkyard.

The ancient Autobot didn't like the fact that his sensors hadn't turned up anything. From extensive experience, he knew that he was in for trouble, that he was about to encounter something not only unexpected, but also very dangerous.

All righty, then, Ironhide thought as he curled the fingers of his right hand into a metal fist.

You wanna play hide-and-seek? I know that game. And I know you're not gonna like it when you lose.

Servos whining, Ironhide broke into a trot among the stacks of crushed vehicles, and he crossed the length of the junkyard in twenty seconds. He reached a gap between a row of junked parts and the surrounding fence and quickly turned his scarred head left, then right. Broken glass and metal glittered in the moonlight, but his scans didn't find anything resembling a caution or a hazard.

Not a single thing worth blasting.

The junkyard was like a huge maze. Ironhide turned right, arm cannons held in front of him. Another long pathway lined with piles of smaller metal scrap awaited him—old washers and dryers, bicycles and shopping carts. The path was broken here and there by spaces big enough for a forklift...or a Cybertronian.

Keep your cool, Ironhide told himself. *It's just like Ky-Alexia, or the Tangles back on Gorlam Prime. Those battles turned out fine.*

Moving quickly, the massive Autobot jogged from row to row, amplifying his sensory input each time he had to peek around the corner of a stack of wrecked parts. Again and again, the outcome was the same. No matter where he looked, he found nothing. Out of sheer annoyance, he almost said out loud, *Come out, come out, wherever you are!*

But then Ironhide heard a faint noise. If he hadn't set his auditory inputs to maximum sensitivity, he would have missed it entirely. He thought it sounded like metal on gravel and dirt, but he couldn't tell which direction it had come from. Only after he turned his head quickly to the right and then left did he realize that the noise must have come from behind him.

A millisecond later, he didn't have any difficulty hearing the roar of a missile launching or sensing that it was approaching fast, straight for the back of his head.

Ironhide threw himself flat against a pile of scrap metal. A brilliant streak of fire burst through the area of space where his head had been just a split second before. The intensity of the missile's trail scrambled his optical sensors, filling them with static and leaving him unable to see clearly, but he heard the missile scream straight into a stack of late-model fender bender victims. The missile detonated, sending shards of metal and glass and plastic flying in all directions.

On second thought, Ironhide mused, *Ky-Alexia was no picnic.*

His leg servos screaming, the Autobot blinked and tried to adjust his vision as he threw himself backward, aiming for whomever or whatever had fired the missile at him. Flipping through the air, he landed on his hands, then shoved off the ground, hoping his feet would connect with his attacker. And when his feet did connect, he felt the satisfying impact of metal on metal, and he instinctively knew that he hadn't just hit a stack of crushed cars.

Found you!

Ironhide bounced off the thing he'd hit, then rolled into an upright position and unleashed his arm cannons to shoot a barrage of projectiles. As he turned and fired, the static faded from his visual field, allowing him to see that his enemy was an unmanned robotic tank with a dull black exterior. And much to his regret, he also saw that his arm cannons had fired too high.

The tank had two treads, one in back and one in front. The armored vehicle was topped with a low turret that held a single long gun barrel. Ironhide automatically scanned the tank, registering that it had a nonreflective surface that gave off minimal heat. The tank was invisible to a wide range of sensors, and it was especially hard to see at night.

Clever, Ironhide thought. *But I see you now!* He opened fire. Although his first cannon shots had missed, his second barrage hit the base of the tank's turret, knocking the tank backward a few feet and leaving dents and scorch marks. But the turret kept turning, trying to put the Autobot back in the tank's sights.

Tough armor. But not this tough! Ironhide

rapidly cycled his weapons, replacing his right arm cannon with a missile launcher. Responding to his electronic command, his forearm's metal parts began to slide and retract as other parts extended, reshaping themselves into a missile-launcher configuration. Unfortunately, his parts were still shifting when the tank fired again.

Ironhide threw himself hard to one side, bracing himself for an explosive impact. But instead of getting what he'd expected, he received another bright flash of fire that blinded him again. He rolled across the dirt, blinking as he tried to put distance between himself and the tank. When his optics cleared a moment later, the tank was gone.

Ironhide looked at the ground and saw tread marks leading off to the left. His sensors determined that the tank had fled in the same direction from which it had come. Missile launcher ready, he followed the tread marks, but they disappeared in a stretch of gravel and dirt that looked completely undisturbed. Only the tank's initial burst of speed had left tracks that Ironhide could follow. He continued to the next gap between junk piles, but the tank was nowhere in sight. Evidently, the tank was as stealthy as it was fast and well armored.

Okay, Ironhide thought, *gotta admit: I'm impressed.*

Wanting to view the area from a higher vantage point, the Autobot diverted maximum power to the servos in his legs and leaped thirty feet into the air, sensors dialed for maximum sensitivity. He spotted the tank moving up another gap between piled junk, but the tank saw him, too, and responded by firing another missile.

The missile zoomed past Ironhide's right shoulder, close enough that he felt the heat from its exhaust. He tumbled to the ground, landed heavily, and prepped his missile launcher as he sprinted around a heap of rusting car doors to emerge at the end of the row where he'd seen the tank. Finding his target, he opened fire, aiming for the turret. He'd expected the tank to take evasive action or to retreat. Instead, the turret plunged swiftly, ducking into its own body as it lurched forward to intercept him. Iron-hide's missiles streaked over the tank's sunken turret and struck a section of the distant fence. As the fence turned into an explosion of smoke and broken, sparking wires, the tank collided with Ironhide's metal midsection, knocking the

Autobot off his feet and onto the tank's black hull.

Ironhide tried to shove himself free from the tank, but his hands only slid against its smooth surface. As he struggled to find a grip, the tank rose up on its back treads, folded its front section down to place the turret on the central front area of its outer frame, and shifted its form so it appeared to be rising to a standing position before it came to a sudden stop. Ironhide fell backward as the tank motored into reverse on its lower treads, pulling away from him. As he rolled across the ground, he glanced at the tank to see that it was readjusting its turret back up to take aim at him.

Before the tank could fire, Ironhide sprang forward and tackled his opponent. He lost his footing in a loose stretch of gravel and wound up being dragged along as the tank continued to scramble in reverse. The tank swerved around a wrecked truck, whose grille clipped the back of Ironhide's left hand. The impact jarred his hand free, and he flailed for a better grip on the tank until his fingers locked onto the turret's long gun barrel.

The tank swung the barrel wildly back and forth, trying to break the Autobot's hold, but Ironhide kept a firm grip as he dug his feet into the ground. The tank's engine whined and groaned as it slowed to a stop.

"Gotcha!" Ironhide yelled.

Small hatches popped open across the tank's hull, exposing several machine guns. The guns fired, spraying bullets at Ironhide's metal body. Ironhide yelled as warnings poured in from his electronic nerves, but then he shut down the warnings because he knew his upper body was fairly well protected, at least for a short time. Bullets continued to bounce off him as he held tightly to the turret's barrel with his right hand. He pushed the barrel as hard as he could, producing a loud groan of stressed metal as he bent it upward.

The tank shuddered. Ironhide kept his grip on the ruined turret as the tank shifted its form so it was once again resting on both treads. Ironhide let go, landing in the gravel to crouch on one knee beside the tank. The tank's turret spun around, but the end of its bent barrel now pointed uselessly at the sky.

Ironhide checked his systems. The machine-gun fire had cut into his upper left arm, but the damage was minor. As Ironhide rose to his feet, determined to finish the fight, the tank suddenly backed away from him.

"Yer going down," Ironhide growled as he

extended his right arm. But then he saw two more hatches open in the tank's upper surface. Out popped a copper-colored dish and a gleaming silver tube. The dish suddenly glowed red, and Ironhide's sensors became instantly overwhelmed by electronic noise. Static simultaneously clouded his vision and screeched through his auditory circuits, overloading them.

Still extending his right arm, Ironhide struggled to focus as he stepped forward and launched a missile. The missile went wide to the right, smashing into car parts and sending them tumbling across the junkyard. As he groped for the tank, he did not see that its silver tube, a directed-energy weapon, had stopped moving, or that it was pointed straight at him. Nor did he hear the humming noise as the weapon activated, but he did feel the intense heat that shot up through his right arm and shoulder, causing his sensors to scream in protest.

"First missiles and machine guns," Ironhide snarled, "and now electronic countermeasures and microwaves? You're full of surprises!" Still blinded, he sprang forward and grabbed the tank. He shoved it with all his might into the nearest pile of junk, half burying it in the scorched wreckage of a utility truck and dislodging the crushed vehicles stacked above the truck. As the tank struggled to free itself from the avalanche, Ironhide shook his head again, shaking off the effects of the tank's electronic weapons. His vision cleared, and he launched one giant foot at the tank's hull to stomp on the copper dish. The dish shattered, and the shrieking in Ironhide's ears stopped.

Ironhide grabbed the tank's microwave cannon and mashed it into scrap. He seized the twisted turret, holding the tank still as he aimed his missile launcher at the seam where the turret joined the hull. A series of beeps and a data readout confirmed he had missile lock—not that he needed any confirmation to hit a target that was only two feet away. He was about to fire a missile when spotlights flared to life on all sides of the junkyard.

"End test!" a man's voice boomed and echoed over the junkyard. "End test!"

Ironhide recognized the voice. "Nothin' doin', General," he said. "I'm in a mood to remodel, and this tank will look a lot better with a big smoking hole in it."

"Ironhide," said another voice. This one was deep and not even slightly human, and it had a tone that betrayed that the speaker was used to others following his orders. "The exercise is complete. Stand down."

Ironhide knew that Optimus Prime wasn't joking. But as he lowered his arm and stepped away from the wrecked tank, he said, "Aw, c'mon, boss. Can't a guy have a little fun?"

Chapter Two
DR. PORTER'S TOY

A canvas-topped military truck sped down the lane among piles of junk, followed by the towering form of Optimus Prime, whose blue armor plating was decorated with red flames. The truck came to a stop, and General Marcus emerged, accompanied by two aides who were followed by a man in a white lab coat. The man in the coat had long gray hair and horn-rimmed glasses.

"Interesting exercise, Ironhide," General Marcus said, blue eyes bright against his tanned face.

"Interesting?" Ironhide shrugged. "I guess that's one way to describe it." He tried not to laugh at the sight of the general's U.S. Army uniform, which he thought looked ridiculous, the way it was covered with insignia, ribbons, and medals. *Why do Earth's military leaders like to decorate themselves with all that stuff?* But Ironhide had to admit that General Marcus was sensible for a human. Ever since Marcus's Army unit had joined forces with the secret military unit known as NEST, an acronym for Non-biological Extraterrestrial Species Treaty, he'd proved himself as a very capable commanding officer. The Autobots and the U.S. armed forces had formed NEST to join their efforts in defending Earth against the Decepticons and their evil leader, Megatron.

General Marcus and the man in the lab coat picked their way across the gravel to arrive beside the smashed tank. Marcus examined the tank's bent gun barrel and let out a low whistle. The man in the lab coat turned to face Ironhide, looked up at the robot, and said angrily, "What part of the words *end test* was unclear to you?"

Ironhide looked away from the man in the lab coat, then returned his gaze to the man's outraged expression and said, "You talkin' to me?"

General Marcus moved beside the man in the lab coat and placed a hand on his shoulder as he looked up at Ironhide. "Ironhide, meet Alexander Porter. Mr. Porter—"

"*Dr.* Porter," the man snapped.

"My apologies," General Marcus said soothingly. "*Dr.* Porter is the president and CEO of Hyperdynamix Laboratories. His laboratory created the prototype you fought tonight."

Ironhide stepped back and bent down to

place his scarred metal face close to Porter's. "Whatsamatter, Doc?" he boomed. "Afraid I was gonna break your toy?"

Not showing a trace of fear or intimidation, Porter replied sharply, "That *toy* costs thirty million dollars. Its turret contains sensitive diagnostic equipment that recorded every second of tonight's test. A missile impact at point-blank range could have destroyed that data. Unless you want to spend every night out here fighting tanks, I suggest that when someone says 'end test,' you *end* the *test*."

Ironhide chuckled as he stood up away from Porter. "If you're so concerned about your precious gadgets, do yourself a favor and send out the next tank with a sign on it that says 'I surrender.'"

Porter's left eye twitched. "You think I'm joking? I doubt you'd be so amused if our tank had been using fully loaded munitions, or if it had its microwave emitter set to full power, or if its systems had been set on full automatic instead of being operated by remote control. If you'd gone up against all *that* tonight, I don't think we'd be having this conversation." Porter smiled. "In fact, I think you'd be dead."

Ironhide moved quickly as he took a heavy step toward Porter, prompting the startled man to take a quick step backward. Staring down at Porter, Ironhide said, "Made you flinch."

Optimus Prime cleared his throat. Ironhide looked away from Porter to see the towering Autobot leader giving him a warning glance.

"Gentlemen," General Marcus said. "Let's remember we're on the same team."

"Of course," Porter said. "I apologize if I got carried away. I take my work very seriously."

"I take *my* work seriously, too, Doc," Ironhide said as he casually punched his right hand into his left palm to make a loud clanging noise. "But I accept your apology." He looked at the ruined tank and added, "Your toy put up a pretty good fight. Any time you're ready for another round, let me know."

"Excellent," General Marcus said. "Well, then, Dr. Porter, let me commend you for an excellent first effort. We all look forward to reviewing the diagnostics and discussing the future direction of your research. I know Hyperdynamix has a lot of work to do before we have an autonomous tank capable of taking on the Decepticons, but it's clear to me that we've taken an important step forward to that goal."

Porter nodded. "General, you know the United States, and all the nations of our world, can depend on my best efforts, as well as those of every Hyperdynamix employee. We will all do whatever we can to help defeat the Decepticons who have invaded our planet." Porter gestured to Ironhide and Optimus Prime as he added, "With the help of our Autobot allies, of course."

"Dr. Porter," Optimus said, "did you say the prototype tank was operated by remote control?"

Porter nodded distractedly as he turned his attention to his tank. "Yes. That's what I said."

Optimus glanced at Marcus, then said, "Who was operating the controls?"

Porter turned to look back at the Army truck. He stuck two fingers into the corners of his mouth and let out a loud whistle. In response, a teenage boy in civilian clothes climbed down from the back of the truck. The boy had a military-grade communications headset perched on his well-groomed blond hair. Facing Dr. Porter, he said, "You didn't have to whistle so loudly."

"Allow me to introduce my son, Douglas," Porter said.

Douglas Porter smiled politely.

Chapter Three
THE SCIENTIST'S SON

"You're Optimus Prime," Douglas said. "And you're Ironhide. It's an honor to meet you both."

Douglas extended a hand to Optimus Prime, who touched it with his fingertip in greeting. Ironhide gave him a quick fist bump, carefully calibrating the impact so he wouldn't shatter the young human's forearm.

"Your reaction time is amazing, Ironhide," Douglas said in admiration. "I thought I had you with that first missile. I don't know how you avoided it."

"It's simple math," Ironhide said with a shrug. "Motion equals survival. If ya stand still, ya get hit!"

Douglas looked at the tank and said, "There's a bit of latency with the remote control—the time it takes for the tank to respond to the commands. We've got the lag time below a third of a second, but we can't get it any lower. When the tank becomes self-directed and fully automatic, its reaction time will be faster."

"Faster?" Ironhide sounded faintly disturbed.

Dr. Porter shot a glance at Douglas and said, "The problem wasn't with the lag time. The problem was the reaction time of the person operating the controls."

Douglas stood very still and shifted his gaze to the ground. "I'm sorry I disappointed you, sir."

"You didn't just disappoint me, Douglas," Porter said. "You *failed* me."

Ironhide looked at Optimus Prime. Optimus said, "Take it easy, Ironhide."

"Like nuts, I will." Ironhide trained his eyes on Dr. Porter and said, "You're a real prince, Doc. I'll bet you take after your own father." As the senior Porter's face went red with a mix of anger and embarrassment, Ironhide reached out to gently nudge Douglas's shoulder and said, "Pay no attention to your old man, kid. You did just fine. Heck, we might make an Autobot outta you. If you were already fourteen feet tall and made of metal, your club membership would be a done deal."

Douglas smiled. "Thank you. That compliment means a lot to me, particularly coming from a legend such as yourself."

General Marcus looked at the teenager and

said, "I thought you performed well, too, Douglas, but..." He shook his head, then turned to Dr. Porter. "I still think your son is a bit young to be fighting giant robots."

Ironhide said, "Too young? What do you mean? Douglas looks like he's older than Kevin."

Douglas said, "Kevin?"

Before Ironhide could reply, Optimus Prime interjected, "Kevin is another friend of ours." Optimus turned to General Marcus and said, "What happens next, General?"

"The technicians are on their way to collect the prototype. Optimus, I have some interesting new satellite data that I think you'll want to see." He looked at Dr. Porter and Douglas. "Shall we call it an evening, gentlemen?"

Dr. Porter shook his head. "*Our* work isn't done. I want to examine my tank before the technicians arrive, and also make sure they don't cause any further damage. Douglas will assist me."

"Very well, Dr. Porter," General Marcus said. "Congratulations again on such a promising first test."

The general and his aides climbed back into the truck. As Optimus and Ironhide headed for the junkyard's exit, Ironhide held out one hand and drummed his knuckles against a series of wrecked cars. He said, "You know anything about the satellite data that Marcus mentioned?"

Optimus shook his head. "We can only assume the data is important." He surveyed the junkyard thoughtfully. "Dr. Porter's dedication to his work seems unquestionable. It is unfortunate that he is not as well-behaved as his offspring."

"Well-behaved? That kid?" Ironhide scoffed. "I thought he was a total suck-up!" He rocked his head back and forth as he mimicked Douglas's voice and said, " 'That compliment means a lot to me, particularly coming from a legend such as yourself.' Think about it, Optimus. No kid talks like that unless he *wants* something."

"Really? And what exactly were you hoping to obtain when you told him he was well on his way to becoming a member of the Autobot club?"

"I just didn't like the way his father talked to him, and I wanted to mess with his old man's head. If you ask me, the father's a jerk and the kid's a sneak."

Optimus turned and regarded Ironhide. "Is this hostility an example of your usual anti-social behavior, or does it have to do with the fact that the boy nearly defeated you?"

Ironhide came to a halt. "Aw, boss, how can you say that? *No one* nearly defeated me! The kid got lucky once!"

"Once?"

"Okay, maybe twice."

Optimus resumed walking, and Ironhide fell into step beside him. Optimus said, "I shall examine the telemetry with great interest."

"I'm tellin' ya, I was taking it easy on him!"

"I'm sure you were," Optimus said. "And I'm sure you would have done more damage, but you didn't want to hurt young Mr. Porter's feelings."

"You got that right, brother," Ironhide said. "I think he's a sneak, but I didn't feel any need to rub his nose in it."

Optimus shook his head. "As always, Ironhide, your thoughtfulness amazes me."

When the two Autobots were gone and the tail-lights of the Army truck had dwindled and disappeared into the night, Alexander Porter turned and jabbed one long finger in Douglas's face. "You were holding back! Why?"

"I wasn't, Dad," Douglas said. "I did my best. Ironhide is tougher and faster than we expected. Smart, too."

"Faster than *you* expected," Porter said. "In the hands of a more experienced controller, our prototype could have leveled that Cybertronian clown!"

"The prototype did well," Douglas insisted. "And remember the lag time. As you said yourself, the tank might have taken down the Autobot if it had been on full power."

"Maybe," Porter said. "I want to step up work on the autonomous programming. We'll start tomorrow morning."

"But...I still have homework to do tonight, and—"

"I said we'll start tomorrow morning!"

"Yes, sir." Douglas looked down at the prototype's twisted gun barrel, still bearing the dents from Ironhide's massive metal fingers. "It'll take a while to get this unit back online."

Alexander Porter smiled. "Not as long as you might think."

"What do you mean?"

"I've already manufactured twelve more units. Look here."

Porter pulled out his smartphone and brought up a video that showed the inside of a hangar. The hangar's walls were marked with a bold red H, the logo of Hyperdynamix. On the hangar's floor, twelve tanks stood at attention while Hyperdynamix technicians inspected their dull black finishes. Porter stopped the video and glared at his son. "If the lag time can't be reduced, everything depends on the autonomous programming. Otherwise, what am I supposed to do with these robot tanks? Scrap them and go back to the drawing board?"

"No, sir," Douglas said. "That won't happen, sir."

"You bet your life it won't."

An hour later, many miles from the military base, Douglas Porter sat in his bedroom, pretending to do his homework. He had received a text message from Charlene Poole, his girlfriend back in Hurley's Crossing. Douglas ignored the message. He had work to do.

Douglas fired up his sleek metal laptop and let his fingers dance over the keys. A few seconds later, he used the computer to place an untraceable call to a cell phone. The phone rang twice before a man picked up and responded, "Go ahead, Stealth Leader!" The man, Simon Clay, had no idea that Stealth Leader was a teenage boy named Douglas Porter, and he was prepared to carry out Stealth Leader's orders because that's what he was paid to do.

Douglas had programmed his computer to disguise his voice. When he began to speak, wavy lines jumped on his screen as the program turned his voice into a deep monotone. "Do you have video from the incident at the Hawthorne Army Depot?"

"Yes, Stealth Leader," Clay said. "Our spy

drones only saw the last part of the battle, but we got enough."

"Transmit it to me now."

"Roger that."

A few seconds passed, and then a jerky video began playing on Douglas's computer. The video was green and fuzzy, shot from above in low light by a drone-mounted night-vision camera. Douglas watched, fascinated, as the Decepticon he knew as Reverb threw a long cylinder into the desert ground, right into the middle of a group of soldiers. Douglas peered at the screen and thought he saw a flicker along the cylinder, which was followed by a blinding flash that washed out the camera's view. When the flash faded, the soldiers were on the ground, shaking uncontrollably. And then they disappeared.

Douglas kept watching. He saw Reverb, his metal body outfitted with strange Cybertronian weapons, fighting against the Autobots known as Ratchet and Bumblebee. Reverb had somehow acquired a protective energy shield, and he was giving the Autobots a thorough pounding. And then Optimus Prime and Ironhide arrived, but they fared no better against Reverb's weapons. All four Autobots were down and the human soldiers were not posing any threat to Reverb.

If the video had ended right there, and if Douglas had not met Optimus Prime and Ironhide earlier that night, he might have assumed that Reverb had won the battle at the Hawthorne Army Depot. But knowing better, Douglas continued watching the video.

The drone's cameras turned to a low dome surrounded by rubble. A Transformer was lying, apparently damaged, in the mouth of a cave. Another Transformer stepped out from the cave, the air shimmering strangely around his body. The new arrival and Reverb appeared to speak to each other. Then the newcomer retreated into the cave. Reverb followed, but he was blasted by the Transformer who lay in the rubble.

The blast shorted out Reverb's weapons. A moment later, Optimus Prime and Ironhide reappeared, apparently having recovered. Reverb fought briefly with Optimus, but the Autobot leader gained the upper hand and drove his massive, retractable metal blade into Reverb's innards. Douglas winced at the sight. And then the fight was over.

But the spy drone kept recording. Douglas frowned as a kid ran out of the cave and dropped to his knees next to the fallen Autobot, the one who'd blasted Reverb. Douglas leaned closer to his laptop's screen.

It can't be, he thought. *It's that Bowman kid. Kevin Bowman.*

Douglas wasn't especially good at remembering names of people he suspected he'd never see again, but he did remember Kevin Bowman. He'd seen Kevin a month earlier at Charlene Poole's birthday party, which Douglas had financed to provide an alibi for his whereabouts that night. According to Charlene, who also knew nothing about Douglas's alter ego, Stealth Leader, Kevin was her brother's friend, not hers. As if Douglas really cared one way or the other.

Douglas had been sitting in Charlene's living room, watching television, when a news station began showing footage of a Decepticon attack on an Air Force base. Douglas had a special interest in watching the footage because Simon Clay, following Stealth Leader's orders, had engineered the attack. But then Kevin Bowman had started talking, said his parents had been killed two years ago in the battle between Autobots and Decepticons that had torn apart downtown Mission City.

Douglas tried to remember how he had responded to Kevin's story, how he had acted. Thinking back, he recalled he'd basically laughed at Kevin and told him that the giant robots didn't really exist. So much for keeping the kid in the dark.

This isn't good, Douglas thought. *This isn't good at all.*

But he could fix it. He was Douglas Porter. He could fix anything.

"Stealth Leader?" Clay said. "Are you still there?"

"Yes," Douglas said. "Get specialists to enhance the video of that cylinder, the thing the robot threw. And then I have a new job for you. It'll be at Hyperdynamix Laboratories."

"Hyperdynamix?" Clay sounded stunned. "But their security is airtight."

"Are you saying you can't do it?"

"I'm saying this job won't come cheap, boss."

"Since when," Douglas said testily, "has cost been an issue with me?"

"Okay, okay," Clay said. "What does the job require?"

Douglas smiled. "Trucks," he said. "You'll need twelve."

Chapter Four
HOMECOMING

Kevin Bowman was home—or, rather, he was in the house that he had once called home. A lot had happened in the past month, and as the twelve-year-old boy looked around the low-slung ranch house in the Nevada desert town of Hurley's Crossing, he realized that home wasn't what it used to be.

A military helicopter had carried Kevin to the house, and the helicopter now rested in the backyard with a waiting pilot. Kevin had lived in the house with his brother, Duane, ever since their parents died two years earlier. Duane had been employed at the Hawthorne Army Depot, struggling to raise his little brother alone. Now Duane was gone, too, having vanished after a close encounter with an ancient Cybertronian cylinder, the one the Decepticon named Reverb had hurled at a squad of soldiers that included Duane.

General Marcus and Optimus Prime had warned Kevin that his brother was most likely dead. Even if Duane had survived contact with whatever strange force field the alien pillar had produced, the cylinder could have transported him anywhere in the universe. And in the vast majority of the universe, the life expectancy of an unprotected human was seconds or less.

Kevin knew General Marcus and Optimus

Prime were right. But despite that, he wouldn't give up hope. He couldn't. Hope was all he had.

Still, hope didn't make it any easier to stand in an empty house where everything reminded him of his brother. Sitting in the kitchen sink was a mug, empty except for a dark crust of old coffee at the bottom. In front of a chair near the TV sat the boots Duane liked to wear while hiking. On the mantel sat a photo of Kevin and Duane from a camping trip last fall. Next to it was a photo of a younger Kevin with a younger Duane, smiling with their parents.

"Hey, kid," said a man behind Kevin, reminding him that the house wasn't entirely empty, that he wasn't completely alone. Kevin turned to look at the pair of NEST commandos who had followed him into the house. The commando who'd just spoken continued. "Our orders are to hurry. We've blocked off the road around the house, but we'd rather not have to explain ourselves to the local authorities."

Kevin stared hard at the commando. "We just got here."

"Sorry," the commando said.

"It's okay," Kevin said, then looked away from the soldiers so they wouldn't see he was blinking back tears. "You're right. We can't stay here. Just let me get my clothes and a few other things."

He walked down the hall to his bedroom. His unmade bed was as he'd left it, with a book propped up on his pillow. To the left of his closet was his grandfather's old stereo system, complete with a turntable and bulky headphones. Duane had helped him set up the stereo, and Kevin could only guess how many hours he'd spent listening to vinyl records. Thinking of this made the silence in the room that much more painful. And because of the silence, and because the house wasn't very large, he could easily hear the commandos' conversation in the kitchen, even though they were trying to keep their voices low.

"Doesn't seem right, dragging a kid into this war with the Decepticons."

"That kid saved a lot of lives at Hawthorne," the other commando said. "His brother's missing or dead, and he's got no other family. The least we can do is help him out."

"I'm with you on that."

"Then let's get to it and get this house secured. Windows closed and locked, trash emptied, and clean out the fridge. You checked the home security system?"

"Everything's wired, and a cleaning crew will be here soon."

"Okay. I want this place looking good as new when the kid returns."

When I return? Listening from his bedroom, Kevin wondered if he would ever come back to Hurley's Crossing. Until he found his brother, he didn't see much point in planning too far ahead.

As Kevin picked up a backpack and moved over to his desk, he heard a mechanical whine outside his window. He looked to the window just as a dark shape blotted out the morning sunlight. Startled, Kevin jumped, then he peered outside. He saw a familiar face that was composed of metal plates.

"Gears!" Kevin shouted. "You scared me half to death!"

The silvery gray Autobot peered curiously into Kevin's bedroom window. "I don't know why you're scared," Gears said. "You do remember I traveled here, don't you?"

"Sure, I remember," Kevin said. "Sorry, I was just thinking about other stuff." Kevin began filling up his backpack with schoolbooks he'd left behind. General Marcus and Optimus Prime had made him agree to regular tutoring sessions.

Watching Kevin, Gears said, "Did I really scare you half to death?"

"Yup, you really did."

Gears activated an instrument within his chest and a blue light flickered over Kevin. Gears said, "My scanners register that you're in good health, without any indication of fifty percent mortality. Are you certain that you've lost half your life expectancy?"

"It's an *expression*, Gears!"

"Oh." Embarrassed, the Autobot flicked his eyes back and forth. "Then I hope you will disregard my last question."

Kevin shook his head, amused. A month earlier, not far from his home, Gears had saved

Kevin's life, catching him after a mysterious speeding van had hit his bike, and then defended him from the Decepticon named Reverb. Kevin had returned the favor during a battle in the desert outside Hawthorne, helping Gears take Reverb by surprise. Gears had been badly damaged in the fight but had since recovered, except for a slight limp that made him favor his left leg. As for Reverb, he was now NEST's prisoner.

Gears cleared his mechanical throat, then said, "Kevin?"

"Yes, Gears?"

"What is your dwelling made out of? It appears to be deceased vegetable matter. Am I correct?"

"Deceased vegetable matter?" Kevin considered Gears's words, then replied, "The house *is* made of wood, so I guess you're right."

"Peculiar," Gears said.

"You think? Why? What was your childhood home made out of?"

"I am not entirely certain," Gears said. "I believe it was a self-replicating nanoceramic matrix around a titanium shell."

"Oh," Kevin said. "That wasn't an option for Duane and me."

"That is understandable," Gears said. "I don't believe such materials are easily available on Earth." Gears shifted his bulk outside the window. "Would you like to play Twenty Questions, Kevin?"

Kevin grinned. He had taught Gears the game after the battle with Reverb, when the Autobot had spent the better part of several days lying very still and letting his damaged systems repair themselves. Gears had enjoyed the game, and he typically asked to play it several times a day.

"Sure, Gears. Let's play. Just remember to keep low so nobody sees you from the road."

"The NEST truck is blocking the view from the road. I am ready, Kevin."

"Okay," Kevin said as he stuffed a week's worth of clothes into an old, worn duffel bag. "Is it animal, vegetable, or mineral?"

"Mineral."

"Is it alive?" Kevin asked. But then he added, "Before I met you and the other Cybertronians, I never would have thought to ask if something mineral was alive."

Gears cocked his head. "That is logical. Your planet's ecology is still primitive when it comes to higher life-forms. The answer to your question is yes; I am thinking of something that is living matter. Or *was* living matter."

Kevin smiled, and Gears grunted in irritation as he realized his mistake. Gears said, "I have accidentally given you the answer to a question you had not yet asked."

"Yup." Kevin cinched up his duffel bag and looked around his room. Posters of his favorite bands were on the wall. A few action figures that he thought he could never part with were on a shelf. A fly-fishing rod that Duane had given him on his last birthday leaned in a corner. *Never even got to use it...*

"Kevin?" Gears said. "It is your turn to ask the next question."

"Sorry, Gears," Kevin said. "Okay, let's see....It's mineral, living matter, but is no longer alive. Gears, I have to ask: Does the answer involve some ancient Cybertronian who I couldn't possibly have ever heard of? Or anything else that I would never find in any textbook on Earth?"

"You cannot do that, Kevin," Gears said.

"According to the rules, as you explained them to me, the game does not permit asking multiple questions during a single turn."

"I'm just trying to save both of us from wasted time and frustration," Kevin said. "I don't mean to pick on you, but more than once, your 'answer' to Twenty Questions has been beyond anything I'll ever know or guess."

Gears thought for a moment, then said, "You have not heard of the Fifth Baron-Warlord of Polyhex, known in the Cybertronian language as…" Gears made a noise like a radio shorting out in a poorly balanced washing machine.

Kevin laughed. "No, Gears. I'm afraid not. Never heard of the guy."

"He is quite famous," Gears said, sounding disappointed. "But I forget that you are an immature human and therefore still poorly educated about history."

"Sorry, Gears," Kevin said with a smirk. He'd already tried to explain to Gears that Cybertronian history was never mentioned in any classrooms on Earth. "I'm going to close the window now. I'll meet you at the truck, okay?"

"I will be waiting for you."

Kevin shut the window, strapped on his backpack, and hefted his duffel bag. He walked out of the bedroom, shutting the door behind him, and proceeded to the living room. There, he found the two NEST commandos, who had finished their work in the kitchen and were waiting for him at the front door.

As he entered the kitchen, the phone on the wall rang. Kevin recognized the caller ID and picked up the phone. "Gilbert?"

"Kevin! You're home! I just saw an army truck outside your place! What's going on?"

Kevin noticed the two commandos looking at him anxiously. "Hang on, Gilbert," he said, then placed one hand over the phone. "It's my friend," he whispered to them.

One soldier looked at his partner and said, "The phone was supposed to be disconnected."

The other soldier kept his eyes on Kevin and said, "Keep it quick." Kevin nodded. Speaking into the phone again, he said, "It's cool you called, but I can't—"

"Oh, man, you had me worried!" Gilbert interrupted. "I got your e-mail that Duane got transferred to another state, and you had to go with him, but I knew you wouldn't just leave without saying good-bye. So, where've you been?"

Kevin knew that General Marcus had generated a cover story so local authorities would not question Kevin's whereabouts. The story was that he and his brother had temporarily left the area because of Duane's work. Kevin was trying to think of what to say to Gilbert when he noticed one commando spinning his finger, gesturing for Kevin to wrap up the conversation.

"I'm sorry, Gilbert," Kevin said. "I... everything's fine, really, but we just stopped by to get a few more things....I gotta go. I promise I'll call you soon. Bye."

"What? But I—"

Kevin hung up the phone and took a last look around. He walked over to the mantel and grabbed the photos of himself and Duane and their parents. He opened his backpack and pushed aside a math book to make room for the photos, then zipped up the backpack and looked at the commandos. One of them said, "You ready?"

"Sure," Kevin said. But as he followed them outside, he wondered just how ready he really was. Ready for another battle like the one at the

Hawthorne Army Depot? Ready to do whatever it took to find his brother? *I'm just a kid.*

Kevin sighted Gears standing beside a military truck. Shifting back and forth on his metal legs, Gears said, "I'm sorry you don't know about the Fifth Baron-Warlord of Polyhex, Kevin. Would you like to play a new game of Twenty Questions?"

"Okay," Kevin said, "but do me a favor and don't think of anything beyond the solar system."

Gears lifted his gaze to the sky, then looked back at Kevin and said, "Which solar system?"

Kevin sighed. "Never mind."

Gears could tell from Kevin's voice that the boy was sad. He looked at Kevin's house and said, "Don't worry, Kevin. We'll find your brother."

Chapter Five
MISSION BRIEFING

NEST's Rapid Response Base was a new facility housed in old hangars on the northern edge of Nellis Air Force Range in southern Nevada. The base was always humming with activity, but on this particular day, the humming was louder than usual. NEST technicians and commandos rushed this way and that through one large hangar, maneuvering around four of their Autobot allies: Optimus Prime, Ironhide, Ratchet, and Bumblebee. The scurrying humans gave the most space to the commanding figure of Optimus Prime and nearly as much to the irascible, scarred Ironhide. The green and yellow armored Autobots Ratchet and Bumblebee, though, had to dodge the occasional NEST soldier who was too busy to watch where he was going.

Hearing heavy footsteps clank into the hangar, the four Autobots turned to see Gears approaching. Kevin ran alongside him, trying to keep up with Gears's stride.

Bumblebee and Ratchet rushed over to meet them. Ratchet, the Autobots' medical officer, said, "Greetings, Kevin. Did you get everything you needed from your house?"

Although Ratchet had tried to make his question sound casual, Kevin had a feeling that Ratchet was really trying to ask if Kevin was okay. Kevin patted his duffel bag and said, "Sure, no problem."

Turning to Gears, Ratchet said, "And how about you, Gears? Is your leg still giving you some trouble?"

"My leg pistons are still mending," Gears said, "but I'm getting around all right."

Bumblebee responded by extending his arms and swaying his hips back and forth as if he were trying to maintain his balance on a surfboard. He activated his radio to broadcast music, and a voice sang, "*I get around!*" Bumblebee's voice box had been damaged, and it remained broken despite Ratchet's best efforts. Deprived of his own voice, Bumblebee usually managed to make himself understood by playing snippets of old songs, TV shows, and movies. Turning to face Kevin, he played a brief bit of an old R&B song to proclaim that being reunited felt so good.

Ironhide rolled his eyes at Bumblebee's

musical selection, then looked at Kevin and said, "Hiya, kid."

Optimus Prime said, "It is good to see you both. And you arrived just in time. General Marcus has something to show us." Optimus turned to a 'soldier standing nearby and said, "Would you please lead the way, Sergeant Cooke?"

Kevin and the Autobots followed Sergeant Cooke to the back of the hangar, where Cooke opened the doors to an enormous conference room. The room had been built to accommodate large military vehicles, but each Autobot still had to duck through the doorway to make his way inside. Despite being the largest of the Autobots, Optimus Prime barely broke his stride as he entered the room. Bumblebee was less graceful, and he clipped the doorway on his way in, which made him blast some static in embarrassment.

Inside the room, General Marcus and a group

of NEST officers sat around a U-shaped table. Sergeant Cooke grabbed a folding chair and set it up for Kevin so he could sit beside Gears. After all the Autobots were settled, Marcus gestured to an aide, who dimmed the lights. A projector was switched on, and the NEST technicians, Kevin, and the Autobots turned to a large screen to see an aerial view of the desert surrounding the Hawthorne Army Depot.

General Marcus said, "We've performed an exhaustive survey of the artifacts found in the Cybertronian storehouse at Hawthorne. We analyzed the entire region, searching for any clues that might have revealed the storehouse's existence."

Watching the screen, Kevin saw colored lines and equations appear over the desert's surface. General Marcus continued, "Our technicians discovered a faint chemical signature associated with the Hawthorne site, one they were unable to attribute to any natural biological or geological process on Earth." Marcus waved at a series of mathematical symbols that had just appeared on the screen. "Don't ask me what all those numbers and jagged lines mean, boys, because I don't understand a lick of it. But what the technicians figured out is that the chemical signature was unique, like a fingerprint, basically."

The screen changed to a new aerial view that displayed mountains, plains, and lakes. Lines and equations rapidly spilled over the view. Marcus said, "At least we *thought* the signature was unique. You see, after we identified the signature, we used spy satellites and drones to search the globe, looking for any similar chemical signatures. Last week, we found a site that's *very* similar, and it's not very far away."

The view zoomed out, and an outline of

Nevada appeared on the screen. A red X began flashing in the center of the northern part of the state.

"X marks the spot of Battle Mountain, Nevada," General Marcus said. "Anybody know it?"

A surprised-looking technician tentatively raised his hand.

"Yes?" Marcus asked.

"Battle Mountain's a mining town, sir. I've been through it. It's got a few restaurants and a small casino. I think there's one stoplight. There's nothing in Battle Mountain, sir."

"That's where you're wrong, soldier," Marcus said. "There most certainly *is* something in Battle Mountain. Or rather, there's something in the Shoshone Mountains nearby."

The view on the screen zoomed in again. An X blinked southwest of the mining town, atop a low mountain. Marcus said, "The site is on a ridge near Antler Peak, above an abandoned gold mine. Surveillance says there's nothing remarkably visible there. You'd pass right by the place if you didn't know better. But the chemical signature is unmistakable." Marcus gestured to Gears. "We know from Gears that the Cybertronians established munitions storehouses on Earth more than nineteen thousand years ago. That fits with what we've learned about the ancient Cybertronians known as the Seekers. Most of the Cybertronian sites have been destroyed by our planet's own geological processes. When Gears arrived on Earth, he had the coordinates for only the storehouse near Hawthorne. But the Battle Mountain storehouse, from what we can tell, is intact and untouched. However, if we can sniff it out, so can the Decepticons."

Kevin raised his hand. General Marcus nodded at him. Kevin said, "General, that chemical signature…does it have anything to do with the cylinder we found at Hawthorne, the Cybertronian pillar that transported my brother and the soldiers someplace?"

Before Marcus could answer, Optimus Prime said, "We do not know that the artifact transported them anywhere, Kevin."

"But we don't know that it *didn't*," Kevin said. "Maybe there's another cylinder at Battle Mountain. Maybe my brother and the other soldiers are *there*, trapped underground. We… *I* have to go there!"

Gears put his big hand gently on Kevin's shoulder. Thinking Gears was trying to make him stop talking, Kevin reached up to shove Gears's hand away, but then Gears surprised him by saying, "I will go with you, Kevin."

"Neither of you is going anywhere," General Marcus said firmly. "You, Gears, are still reconfiguring your damaged systems. And you, Kevin Bowman, though a very brave and determined young fellow, are still just twelve years old."

Kevin started to protest, but General Marcus held up his hand for silence. Marcus continued. "NEST is definitely going to Battle Mountain. Optimus Prime has orders for those of you selected for this mission. We'll leave in the morning. I don't think I need to tell you that this operation must be conducted with absolute—"

The room's doors flew open, and all heads turned to a frantic-looking aide, a man named Leitch, who had one hand clutching his headset. Marcus said, "What is it, Leitch?"

"Emergency alert, sir!" Leitch said. "The Decepticons are attacking Hyperdynamix Laboratories!"

Chapter Six
DECEPTICON ATTACK!

The Autobots stood back while most of the soldiers in the NEST conference room began talking at once. A few soldiers sprang to their feet too quickly and bumped into one another. Seated in the middle of the tumult, General Marcus remained eerily calm, his fingers casually steepled on the table before him.

"Gentlemen," Marcus said, but when that failed to get his men's attention, he repeated more loudly, "*Gentlemen!*"

The buzz of voices ceased, and heads turned to face Marcus. As the soldiers who'd jumped up from their chairs sat down again, Marcus continued. "Now, then, let's see what we're dealing with, shall we? Collier, get a satellite view of Hyperdynamix on this screen. Then start collecting any other data we can get."

Collier busied himself with his laptop, calling up an overhead view of Mission City, which was located in southern Nevada near Las Vegas. Kevin tensed as Collier zoomed in on the city's southeastern outskirts, the area where his parents had been killed in a battle between Autobots and Decepticons. The U.S. military had kept the battle hushed up until the fact that alien robots had arrived on Earth could no longer be denied.

"Bringing up a live feed now, General," Collier said. On the screen, a plume of smoke hid the center of the Hyperdynamix complex, obscuring much of the view. The complex was as large as a medium-size town. Police helicopters buzzed around the outer perimeter, hesitant to approach any closer.

Leitch adjusted his headset and cupped his hand over one ear. "General, we have a priority communication. It's Dr. Porter from Hyperdynamix."

"Put him through," Marcus said. "Dr. Porter, this is General Marcus. Are you safe?"

"Marcus!" Porter yelled, his voice overloading the speakers. "You have to help us. We count three Decepticons. They've taken down our security systems and are somewhere inside my facility."

"Do you have a fix on their positions, Doctor?"

"No, they knocked out all the security

cameras," Porter said. "They could be any-where. We're blind down here, General!"

Keeping his voice calm, Marcus said, "Are you in a secure location, Doctor? You must give top priority to the safety of your employees."

"We have bigger problems," Porter said. "I think the Decepticons are trying to steal the automated tanks. We can't let the Decepticons take the tanks or the...other technologies we've developed."

Marcus scowled. "What other technologies, Doctor?"

"This line isn't secure. I'd better not say."

"Very well, Doctor," Marcus said as he drummed his fingers on the table. "I want you and your people in a safe location. If you can get out, that's best. If not, hole up where you are and wait for our assistance. Marcus out."

The general examined his knuckles, and for

a moment, strain and doubt showed on his tanned face. But a second later, the expression was gone, and Marcus looked focused and determined as usual. "Optimus," he said. "My mission assessment is that we can't let Megatron add Hyperdynamix's technologies to his growing arsenal. I don't know what else Porter has in his labs that he's so worried about, but I don't want to find out by having it aimed at me. I say we postpone the Battle Mountain mission until Hyperdynamix is secured. Do you agree?"

Optimus ran his metal fingers over his gleaming chin, and Kevin wondered where the mighty Autobot had picked up such a human gesture. Optimus said, "I agree, General, but I am concerned that this attack might be intended to distract us from another, like the feint at Area Fifty-One."

"We have no reason to suspect that the

Decepticons know the secret of Battle Mountain," Marcus said. "It was hard enough for us to discover. Still, we shall leave units here, just in case." Marcus rose, and the NEST commandos hurriedly got to their feet. Marcus continued. "Optimus, I will accompany you, Ironhide, and Ratchet to Hyperdynamix, along with a NEST detachment. Gears and Bumblebee, you'll remain here and monitor conditions at Battle Mountain. If anything changes, take appropriate action."

Marcus's steely eyes swept the room. Kevin looked down at the floor, feeling insignificant and out of place. Marcus said, "Kevin, our science lab chief, Lindsay, has been studying the Hawthorne cylinder. I know he would welcome any insights you and Gears might have into how it functions." Without taking his eyes off Kevin, Marcus said, "Leitch, get Kevin and

Gears the appropriate clearance, effective immediately."

"Yes, General."

"Kevin, I trust you won't neglect your studies?"

Kevin stared at General Marcus in astonishment. Just a few miles away, Decepticons were threatening to get their hands on exotic weapons. Yet at the moment, Marcus's attention was on Kevin and his homework. Kevin felt his face flush as he nodded in response.

"Good," Marcus said with a smile, then looked around the room. "Anyone else have any questions? No? Then let's move out."

Chapter Seven
ALIEN ARTIFACT

Optimus Prime, Ironhide, Ratchet, and dozens of NEST commandos boarded the massive transport helicopters that were waiting outside NEST headquarters, and they lifted off, heading for Mission City. After the helicopters were gone, the base fell quiet. A few technicians peered into their radarscopes, tracking the choppers as they moved south.

While Bumblebee went outside to patrol, Gears and Kevin watched the technicians.

Gears said, "You should do your homework, Kevin."

"I'll get to that later," Kevin said. "First I want a look at the Cybertronian cylinder." He stepped away from Gears and then broke into a fast trot to the exit, which brought him to a long corridor. He ran down it, heading for the science lab, which was at the other end of the NEST base.

"Wait, Kevin," Gears called. "This corridor is too narrow for me to —"

"Stop making excuses and try to keep up!" Kevin called back without breaking his pace. Spotting a directional sign that instructed him to turn right for the science lab, he rounded a corner and ran faster. He sailed through a doorway and into another corridor.

The lab's entrance was at the end of the corridor. A soldier wearing a headset and carrying a machine gun stood outside the entrance. Seeing Kevin running toward him, the guard kept his weapon pointed carefully at the floor and said, "This is a restricted area."

Kevin came to a stop in front of him. "I have clearance. My name is Kevin Bowman."

"*You* have clearance?" The soldier shook his head in obvious disbelief. "Let me guess, kid; you're a general?"

Kevin sighed. "General Marcus told his aide, Leitch, to give me clearance for the science lab. If you'll just check with—"

"Are you pulling my leg?"

"Why would I do that?" Kevin said impatiently. "I mean…I'm already cleared to be inside the base, aren't I? How do you think I got here, a school field trip?"

"Don't get smart with me, kid," the guard said. "If I find out you're messing with me, you're gonna regret—" The commando was interrupted by the sound of loud, clanking footsteps, and then he saw Gears approaching through the corridor.

"Kevin, please don't run off again," Gears said. "In hurrying after you, I stepped on a portable radar installation. The watch officer's aggravation was significant."

"This is Gears," Kevin said as he jabbed a thumb casually over his shoulder. "He's with me. He has clearance, too."

The commando, wide-eyed, spoke briefly into his headset, listened, and then stepped aside for the boy and the giant robot. As Kevin and Gears walked past him and entered the lab, the commando muttered, "First I'm a doorman for robots, and now kids. This is definitely not what I signed up for."

Inside the lab, Kevin and Gears found Chief

Lindsay and a trio of technicians sitting, surrounded by a jumble of laptops, folders, papers, wires, and devices that Kevin couldn't identify. At the center of the lab stood an eight-foot-tall cube made of three-inch-thick glass. Inside the cube, festooned with cables and sensors, stood the ancient cylinder of dark metal that Kevin had last seen stuck in the desert floor at Hawthorne.

Without looking away from his laptop's monitor, Lindsay said, "I've been expecting you two. Gears, I don't suppose you've brought a full schematic of the pillar?"

Gears said, "I am sorry to disappoint you, Chief Lindsay, but my programming does not indicate such a schematic exists."

Lindsay smiled. "I was joking."

"Oh," Gears said. "In that case, I am amused."

He peered through the glass cube to examine the Cybertronian artifact. "Has Reverb supplied any useful information?"

"No," Lindsay said. "Not unless insults and threats are useful."

"In my experience, they are generally not," Gears said. "They are typically just extraneous—"

"Whoa, back up," Kevin said. "Chief Lindsay, you've been talking with Reverb? He's *here*?"

"Oh, yes, he's right down the hall." Lindsay turned from his laptop and smiled at Kevin. "Don't worry. He's triple-manacled, his sonic cannon has been jammed with sound baffles, and he's under around-the-clock guard by commandos with EMP cannons. The moment he misbehaves, he'll be one big short circuit."

Kevin thought it was a bad idea for NEST to be keeping Reverb so close to the ancient cylinder, but all he could do was hope they had the situation under control. He looked at the artifact and said, "So, have you learned anything about the cylinder?"

"To be precise," Gears added brightly, "is it animal, vegetable, or mineral?"

"Oh, definitely mineral," Lindsay said. "It's a metallic alloy…lightweight but extremely strong. There's an internal structure we can't view, even with our most powerful instruments. All we know is the internal structure is somehow connected to those bumps on the surface there."

Kevin looked through the glass and saw four small slightly raised rectangles on the cylinder's surface. As Gears clanked up beside him, Kevin said, "Do you have any idea what the bumps are for?"

"I was hoping Gears might know," Lindsay said, "but for now, we can only guess. Power terminals, maybe. Or readouts. Or serial numbers. Or just decorations. They show evidence of very recent heat damage, though."

Kevin said, "Maybe from when Reverb used this thing on my brother?"

"There could be a connection," Lindsay said. "Kevin, you saw the cylinder in the storehouse before it was used. Do you remember seeing these markings? Did they look different?"

"I didn't notice them," Kevin said. "I'm sorry. There was a lot going on."

"I understand," Lindsay said. "Gears?"

The Autobot paused. Kevin looked at him hopefully.

"My visual memory was damaged in the fight," Gears said. "The missing sectors cannot be reconstructed."

"That is unfortunate," Lindsay said. "But I do have a theory about what this thing is."

Both Kevin and Gears looked away from the cylinder to stare at the scientist. Lindsay continued. "In the second Witwicky incident, the one that culminated in the battle in Egypt, we learned of the existence of an ancient order of Cybertronians who called themselves Seekers," Lindsay said.

"The Wit-what?" Kevin asked.

"Wit*wicky*," Lindsay said. "Sam Witwicky. He's...well, let's just say he's a friend. Like you. And according to him, one of these ancient Seekers was able to teleport himself, along with four humans and three Autobots, from North America to Egypt. The Seeker called this method of travel trans-spatial porting and said it was an ancient Cybertronian technology, one that proved so dangerous that it was abandoned."

"You think that's what this cylinder did?" Kevin asked. "You think it *did* transport my brother to another location?"

Lindsay nodded. "That's exactly what I think."

"Well, if the Seeker knows about ancient technology, why don't you ask him?"

"Regrettably, he didn't survive the Egypt incident."

"Oh. But...there must be a way to find out more! Are there other Seekers we could ask?"

"That's...classified," Lindsay said. "I'm sorry, son. I don't mean to discourage you, but...all I can say is that if there *are* any Seekers out there, there aren't any who could help us with *this*."

"I understand...I guess," Kevin said. "The

people, the four humans who were teleported by the Seeker to Egypt... did they all survive?"

"Yes."

"So if that's what the cylinder did, my brother and those other soldiers must have survived, too, right?"

Lindsay frowned and lifted a hand in caution. "*If* that's what this thing really did. *If* it wasn't malfunctioning. And *if* it sent them somewhere with a breathable atmosphere. I can think of a few dozen more *if*s, but I think you get the idea."

Gears said, "A lot of ifs."

"Exactly," Lindsay said.

"I understand," Kevin said. But somehow, in his heart, he was sure Duane Bowman hadn't been vaporized, that the cylinder had sent his brother through some kind of portal. And Kevin knew that unless Duane had been catapulted directly into a sun, Duane would have found a way to survive whatever was on the other side of that portal.

"My brother's alive," Kevin said. "I know it. And I'll bet that right now, he's doing whatever he can to return here or contact us."

And then Kevin's cell phone rang.

Chapter Eight
AN UNEXPECTED VISITOR

As Kevin fumbled to free the phone from his pocket, he wanted desperately to see his brother's name on the phone's screen. But when he did look at it, instead of the words DUANE BOWMAN, he saw UNKNOWN CALLER. His hand trembled slightly as he said, "Hello?"

"Kevin? It's Douglas Porter."

Douglas Porter? It took a moment for Kevin's addled brain to conjure up who Douglas Porter was, and when he did remember the rich kid whom he'd last seen at Charlene Poole's birthday party, he thought, *Why is he calling me?*

"Kevin, you there?" Douglas said. "We have to talk."

Lindsay and Gears looked at Kevin curiously. Kevin shook his head as he made a sweeping gesture with his hand, signaling to them that the call probably wasn't important. He said, "How did you get my number?"

"The same way I get any number," Douglas said. "Very easily."

Kevin grimaced. He should have expected such a remark from a rich kid with perfect hair and gobs of money and an important father and...

Dr. Porter, Kevin thought, and he felt stupid for not making the connection earlier. He said, "Douglas, are you okay? I know...I mean, I heard that your father's company, Hyperdynamix, was being attacked by—"

"I know about it," Douglas said. "Don't worry about me; I'm somewhere safe. But listen, Kevin, I owe you an apology. I was a huge jerk the last time we met. You remember, at Charlene's party?"

Kevin was faintly amazed that Douglas Porter even remembered his girlfriend's little brother's friend being at the party, let alone the fact that he was calling to apologize. Kevin said, "Yeah, I remember."

"Well, I'm really sorry, Kevin. I didn't want to act that way. But you have to understand that I had secrets to protect. I know a lot about the war between the Autobots and the Decepticons. Working for my father at Hyperdynamix, I've learned secrets that can never be revealed, because those secrets could put everybody on Earth in danger."

If Kevin had heard Douglas make that claim a month ago, he would have assumed that Douglas was just bragging. Although he allowed the possibility that Douglas was telling the truth, he remained suspicious. He said, "Like, what secrets are you talking about?"

"I can't tell you that on the phone. We need to meet."

"That's not going to be easy. I'm not in Hurley's Crossing."

"I know you aren't," Douglas said. "You're at the NEST Rapid Response Base, the new one that NEST and the Army just established at Nellis Air Force Range. It's off the Chalk Mountain route, near State Route 375. That's classified information, of course."

Kevin was stunned. "How do you know…? No, wait, if you say, 'Very easily' again, I'm hanging up."

Douglas laughed. "Actually, there's a simpler explanation. I know all about the base because I was there with my father yesterday. Now, let's meet."

"Okay," Kevin said. "When and where?"

"How about now?" Douglas said. "I'm right outside."

Indeed, Kevin and Gears found Douglas Porter waiting outside at the security checkpoint in front of the main doors to the NEST hangar. Porter was facing two wary-looking NEST guards. Behind Porter, a sleek silver helicopter, gleaming in the last colors of the sunset, rested on the pitted tarmac. A man in a black jacket sat behind the helicopter's controls. Bumblebee stood beside the helicopter's tail boom, tapping the tail rotor with his finger to make it spin faster.

Catching sight of Kevin and Gears, Bumblebee walked over to them as he broke into an old R&B tune about the world being a ball of confusion. Kevin wasn't familiar with the song, but as he looked at Douglas, he did feel confused by the young millionaire's presence.

Douglas gestured to the battered old hangar as he faced Kevin and said, "You're staying *here*?"

"Why not?" Kevin said. "It's not as if my parents have any say in the matter."

Douglas bit his lower lip, then replied, "I said

I was sorry, Kevin. And I really am sorry about your loss." Gesturing to the hangar again, he added, "I didn't mean to sound like...I was just surprised that NEST lets you stay at the base."

Kevin looked to the ground, scuffing at the tarmac with his toe as he tried to get a grip on himself. He didn't want Douglas—perfectly groomed, obscenely rich Douglas—to think he was just some poor kid.

"It's not so bad here," Kevin said. Then he looked at Gears and added, "But it is kind of weird having giant robots insist you do homework."

Douglas grinned and nodded. "That would motivate me!"

Kevin smiled back. He wondered if Douglas might not be so awful after all.

Douglas asked, "Can we go inside? Getting kind of chilly out here."

Kevin turned to the guards. One guard said, "Douglas Porter's Hyperdynamix clearance is still valid. He can enter." The guard waved Douglas in. Douglas walked alongside Kevin as they led Gears and Bumblebee through the hangar's broad doors.

Inside, they found technicians busily studying monitors. Douglas stopped beside a technician's workstation, turned to Kevin, and said, "I know what happened at Hawthorne. You and Gears are heroes."

"Thanks," Kevin said, flushing with embarrassment.

"But the fight is hardly over. Even as we speak, the Decepticons are attacking my father's company's complex."

"They're trying to get the automated tanks, right?"

"That's only part of their plan. One of the things we make at Hyperdynamix is called a communications sniffer. It's a device designed to monitor communications frequencies used by Cybertronians. And it's turned up some very interesting data in the last few days. I brought a recording." Douglas reached into his jacket pocket and extracted several small, expensive-looking gadgets, laying them on the tech's work-station. One of the gadgets was a glossy black cell phone.

"What kind of phone is that?" Kevin asked, curious.

"Hyperdynamix model," Douglas said. "If you're wondering how much it costs, you can't afford one."

"Oh," Kevin said, too fascinated by the

phone to feel insulted. "What about that other thing, the little silver one?"

"That?" Douglas smiled. "Just an MP3 player. A gift from one of my father's business associates. Got enough memory so you can listen to stuff in lossless format, plus it puts out a lot better bass than the phone. Gotta have tunes, right?"

"Yeah, I guess."

"Right. Now listen to this." Douglas tapped on the phone a few times, and it made squalling metallic sounds. The noise meant nothing to Kevin, but Gears cocked his head curiously, and Bumblebee began jumping up and down, randomly playing snippets of songs as he looked for the right one to get his message across.

When the metallic sounds ended, Kevin said, "What was that?"

"Certainly got your friends excited, didn't it?" Douglas said. "None of our analysts at

Hyperdynamix can speak Cybertronian. The language is really complex; some of it is inaudible to our ears, and both Autobots and Decepticons often encrypt their transmissions to guard against eavesdropping. But we have a limited vocabulary figured out, and one thing we understand is Cybertronian numbers."

Gears said, "Kevin, I think we should discuss—"

"Hang on a sec, Gears," Kevin said. "Go on, Douglas."

"Those sounds you just heard aren't random numbers, but geographic coordinates, the Cybertronian equivalents of longitude and latitude. They were transmitted to central New Mexico this afternoon and received by a Decepticon named Blowback. These coordinates are where Blowback is headed right now."

Douglas looked up at Gears and Bumblebee and said, "Either of you ever heard of Blowback?" The two Autobots shook their heads.

Gears's voice sounded tight with concern as he said, "Kevin, Douglas is correct that these are Cybertronian coordinates. I have translated them to your Earth system, and they match the coordinates given during the briefing with General Marcus. The coordinates are for the site outside Battle Mountain."

"Oh, no," Kevin said. "We have to tell Optimus!" Kevin started waving his hand to get a technician's attention, but Douglas grabbed Kevin's wrist.

"Kevin, wait!" Douglas said urgently. "Please...don't."

Baffled, Kevin looked at the older boy. "Why not? NEST thinks the Battle Mountain site is another Cybertronian storehouse, like the one at Hawthorne."

Douglas nodded. "That's what our people at Hyperdynamix think it is, too."

"So we have to tell them!" Kevin said. "We have to send them to Battle Mountain before Blowback gets there!"

Douglas Porter's eyes welled up, and his lower lip began to tremble. For a moment, Kevin thought Douglas was going to burst into tears. But then Douglas blinked furiously, took a deep breath, and got control of himself. "If they come back," Douglas said, "who's going to make sure my father's okay? And what about all the people who could be hurt in Mission City?"

Kevin had been so focused on searching for any link to his lost brother, he had forgotten that Duane's life wasn't the only one at stake.

He suddenly wondered how many families might be affected by the battle in Mission City. "Okay," he said, "let's think this out, Douglas. You said the people at Hyperdynamix think Battle Mountain is another old Cybertronian storehouse. Do they know what's inside?"

"No. We have no idea. Why do you ask? Doesn't NEST have any ideas about what's inside?"

"They don't, but I do." Kevin tried to keep his voice from shaking. "At Hawthorne, the Decepticon named Reverb used an ancient pillar to teleport my brother and those men somewhere. I think it sent them to Battle Mountain, to the other storehouse. I think they're trapped there."

Gears said, "Kevin, you are aware that there is insufficient evidence to support that conclusion."

"Insufficient evidence, huh?" Douglas said. "It sounds plausible to me. And if you're right, we need to hurry. If your brother and the others survived being transported to a chamber inside the mountain…well, that was a month ago. They could be starving to death."

Now even more concerned, Kevin asked, "So what should we do?"

"The way I see it, we have a problem. My father is in one place and needs help. Your brother is in another place—quite possibly the Battle Mountain site—and needs help. And Optimus Prime can't be in two places at once."

"What are you suggesting, Douglas?"

"One Decepticon is headed for Battle Mountain. But we have *two* Autobots, plus whatever you and I can do. We have the Decepticon outnumbered."

Bumblebee had heard enough. He started

jumping up and down, swinging his fists like a boxer, and blasting kung fu movie music.

Douglas continued. "If we're going, we need to leave right now. We might still have a chance of reaching Battle Mountain before Blowback."

Gears said, "I agree with Douglas." Turning his head to regard his fellow Autobot punching at the air, he added, "And with Bumblebee."

"Okay!" Kevin said. "We just need to tell Optimus and General Marcus."

Douglas Porter shook his head. "Bad idea."

Kevin was surprised. "What? But...we can't just *leave*!"

"How do you think they'll react? Oh, I can hear Optimus Prime now. He'll say, 'Good thinking, boys! You two run along with Bumblebee and Gears and fight a Decepticon, and we'll all catch up later.' C'mon, Kevin, you know better than that."

"You're right," Kevin said. "They'd just tell us to stay here."

Douglas nodded. "That's right. Everybody always tells me I'm too young to do stuff I've already proved I can do. It drives me crazy! And if they say that to *me*, what are they going to say to you? You're only what, fourteen?"

"Twelve."

"Even worse, then."

Bumblebee's speakers squealed, and he played a recording of General Marcus from earlier in the evening: "*Gears and Bumblebee, you'll remain here and monitor conditions at Battle Mountain. If anything changes, take appropriate action.*"

Gears said, "I do not think General Marcus was suggesting we leave the base."

Bumblebee folded his arms and activated his

speakers again. Marcus's voice repeated, "...*take appropriate action.*"

Gears said, "I have already processed that data."

"...*take appropriate action,*" Marcus's voice said again.

"You have made your position clear, Bumblebee," Gears said. "Blowback is only one Decepticon. I have faced worse odds."

Kevin said, "That's a yes, then? We're gonna do this?"

Douglas smiled and nodded, then gathered up his gadgets from the workstation. Bumblebee immediately ran for the door, the impact of his footsteps setting the techs' workstations shivering slightly. Gears followed him at a slower pace, with Kevin rushing after.

But Douglas had not taken all of his gadgets.

The little silver MP3 player remained on the workstation, and the vibrations of Bumblebee's footsteps caused the MP3 player to bounce and fall off the edge of the workstation and land on the floor, in the shadows beneath the desk.

Chapter Nine

HIDE-AND-SEEK

"Are the doors secure?" Alexander Porter barked.

"Magnetically locked, sir," replied a Hyperdynamix technician.

"Good," Porter said. "Status of the backup power generators?"

"I just need a minute, Dr. Porter," said another employee, typing furiously.

Only red emergency lighting illuminated Hyperdynamix's control room. Porter and his technicians had fled there after the three

Decepticons cut the power to the complex, leaving them blind. Once inside, Porter had allowed himself to relax a bit. The control room was designed to withstand anything short of a nuclear blast. Even Cybertronian weapons would need hours to drill through its titanium defenses.

But that didn't make Porter feel any better about what might be happening *outside* those doors. Hyperdynamix was a maze of research and development laboratories, weapons-testing chambers, and data warehouses full of information about Autobots and Decepticons, as well as about the weapons systems and technological capabilities of Earth's most powerful nations. The thought of living robots wreaking havoc with any of it made Porter feel sick to his stomach.

"Backup power starting up, sir."

A moment later, the overhead lights flickered and then came back to life, along with the computer screens. Porter yelled, "I want security-camera feeds and status first!"

"Working on it," the technician said, fingers flying over his keyboard. An overhead screen lit up, and images began zipping by from all over the complex, broken up by patches of darkness. "We're dark a lot of places, sir," the tech said, frowning. "But the R and D labs are secure. Same for the weapons-testing facilities."

"Strange," Porter said. "Any word on the servers?"

"Physical facilities are secure," another tech said. "No evidence of computer intrusion. Logs show repeated break-in attempts in other computer systems, but not in the data warehouses."

"Get me full logs," Porter ordered. "And add even more layers of encryption to the firewalls on the data warehouses. Cybertronians can break our encryption schemes very quickly."

"Yes, sir."

Porter scowled at the security-camera feeds on the monitor. "Go back," he said. "Show me the automated-tank ready room."

"Accessing it, sir," a tech said.

Watching the monitor, Porter saw the interior of the tank ready room. He gaped. Instead of seeing twelve prototype tanks, he saw a clear view of the room's bare walls with the red Hyperdynamix logo on them. The room was completely empty.

"Gone!" Porter yelled. "They got all twelve!"

"But sir, the doors are intact," a technician objected. "There's no evidence of any break-in."

"The evidence is right in front of you," Porter said angrily. "No tanks! I don't know how those metal marauders pulled it off, but they did!"

"But then...why are the Decepticons still here, sir?"

Porter thought that was a very good question. If the Decepticons had invaded the complex to steal his tanks and the tanks were gone, why hadn't the Decepticons already left? Why would they risk a confrontation with Optimus Prime and his Autobots?

"I don't know," Porter admitted. "Get me Optimus Prime."

Miles away from Hyperdynamix headquarters, Simon Clay decided it was time to report to Stealth Leader. Clay activated his encrypted satellite phone. Stealth Leader's line rang once and then went silent.

A full minute passed before Clay's phone buzzed. He had received a text message from Stealth Leader, a single word: REPORT.

PHASE I COMPLETE, Clay typed. PHASE II PROCEEDING. UNITS REQUESTING WITHDRAWAL. OPTICIAN IN COMPLEX. He looked at his screen and groaned. But it was too late.

OPTICIAN? Stealth Leader asked.

DARN AUTOCORRECT, Clay wrote. I MEANT OPTIMUS. OPTIMUS AND AUTOBOTS IN COMPLEX. OUR UNITS ASKING TO WITHDRAW.

NO, Stealth Leader replied. KEEP AUTOBOTS BUSY. PLAN DEPENDS ON IT. SL OUT.

"Come out, come out, wherever you are!" Ironhide yelled. He knew that yelling wasn't a good idea, but he'd spent entirely too much time recently wandering around Nevada stalking enemies. He was getting frustrated.

The Hyperdynamix complex was huge and

dark. Somewhere inside were three Decepticons, but Ironhide didn't know where, and his sensors were telling him nothing. Periodic transmissions indicated that Ratchet was having no luck, either, though Ironhide doubted he was as upset by it. Ratchet was a capable warrior, but he still considered himself primarily a medic, and it pained him to snuff out the Spark of any Cybertronian, even a Decepticon's.

Ironhide wasn't troubled by such concerns. The Decepticons had been free to choose their path in life, and they'd chosen to stand against freedom, justice, and peace. The way Ironhide saw things, the Decepticons were targets that had it coming. He was looking forward to giving his best and most explosive regards to the very next Decepticon who made the mistake of stepping into his gunsights.

Ironhide reached another intersection in the

complex and raced across it, forearm cannons aimed left and right, his scarred head whipping in both directions. He found nothing unusual. The intersection was empty, just like every other area of the Hyperdynamix complex that he and Ratchet had explored.

"*What are ya, scared?!*" Ironhide yelled. He'd hoped for an answering roar of defiance or cough of weapons, but all he heard was his own shout, echoing mockingly down the dark corridors.

Very frustrating, Ironhide thought.

"Any success?" General Marcus asked as he looked up to Optimus Prime, who stood next to him outside Hyperdynamix headquarters.

Optimus Prime shook his giant metal head.

"Ironhide and Ratchet are continuing to search the complex. The Decepticons are not engaging. We can only assume they are hiding."

"Ironhide must be beside himself," Marcus said with a small smile.

Optimus nodded. "His preference has always been for action."

"General!" a NEST commando called. "It's Dr. Porter again!"

"Put him through," Marcus said as he raised his phone to the side of his head. "Dr. Porter, are you safe? Good. What's that? Uh-huh. I agree, Doctor.... It is indeed a curious situation. Let me consult with Optimus. Don't worry, Dr. Porter. We'll stop them."

Marcus explained the situation to Optimus Prime. When Marcus was done, Optimus said, "I shall send Ironhide to guard the R and D labs, while Ratchet keeps watch on the weapons-testing department. Can you assign some commandos to the data warehouse?"

"Of course," Marcus said. "I don't understand what the Decepticons' objective is."

Optimus was silent for a moment, then said, "Neither do I."

Chapter Ten
JAILBREAK!

Outside NEST's Rapid Response Base, Bumblebee's metal body was contorting and altering in a flurry of whirling yellow-and-black limbs. When he was finished, a powerful-looking yellow sports car waited on the tarmac, engine purring like a jungle cat.

"Cool," said Douglas Porter.

"It is, isn't it?" said Kevin.

Gears's metal limbs were folding in on themselves, too. A moment later, the Autobot had changed into a battered SUV that had more rust than paint. Seeing Gears's SUV incarnation, Douglas's eyes went wide with surprise. He said, "You can be any vehicle in the world, and you want to be this...this *bucket*?"

Bumblebee spun around, tires smoking, so his headlights faced Gears's mangy vehicular form. His engine thrummed in what sounded suspiciously like a chuckle.

Kevin knew from experience that Gears's car form ran quite smoothly, but he had to admit he wasn't looking forward to crossing Nevada in a vehicle that looked like it was about to fall apart. He said, "Gears, can't you pick something better this time?"

The window of the SUV lowered and the stereo speakers broadcast Gears's voice. "Is there a desired alternative?"

"How about a Lamborghini?" Douglas asked

eagerly. "Or a Porsche? I bet you'd make an excellent Ferrari!"

"I am not familiar with those vehicles," Gears said. "One moment."

The SUV sprouted a head and arms and legs, its old-looking tires migrating to Gears's shoulders as he resumed his bipedal form. Two long strides brought him to the parking lot where a number of vehicles sat waiting. He said, "I see several military transports."

Kevin said, "We need a civilian vehicle, Gears."

Gears continued to survey the parked vehicles until his eyes came to rest on a silver sports car that was more than four decades old. A blue light projected from his eyes as his sensors played over the car, recording its specifications for trans-scanning.

"All right!" Douglas said. "That's a vintage

collector's car! Seriously old-school classic. I bet it belongs to General Marcus himself."

Gears contorted his metal body, and a moment later a replica of the sleek sports car sat in front of them, its engine humming.

Douglas said, "Now, *this* I gotta drive!" He walked around the car and climbed into the front left seat as Kevin entered through the right. Both Douglas and Kevin were surprised to find the steering wheel in front of Kevin.

"What the —?" Douglas said as he examined the car's interior. "Oh, of course. It's a British model, with right-side drive. Kevin, let's switch places so I can —"

"I will drive myself," Gears said firmly, and the car doors' locks clicked. "Bumblebee will lead the way, hopefully at a rate of speed that is not too excessive. Please fasten your safety belts."

Bumblebee pulled away with a squeal of

brakes, his taillights dwindling until they were red pinpricks. Gears fired up his own engine and raced after Bumblebee.

"It is some four hundred miles to Battle Mountain," said Gears as he zipped through the Nevada darkness. "I suggest that the two of you sleep. You will need to be fully recharged when we reach our destination. Besides, you are both immature humans, and your resources are needed for continuing the maturation process."

"In other words, we're growing boys," Douglas said, tapping on his cell phone.

Kevin glanced at Douglas. "What do you keep doing on your phone?"

"Nothing," Douglas snapped as he shifted

his phone so Kevin couldn't see what was on the screen. "I'm just checking in with Hyperdynamix."

Kevin looked out the window. "I don't think I can sleep." He wished there were a way to send a message to his brother, to tell Duane he was coming as quickly as he could.

"Me, neither," Douglas said. "Maybe Gears could tell us a bedtime story."

"Hmm," Gears said. "Do you know the chronicle of Dorsata Secundus, grand commander of the Apex Legions, and the Polis Station Infiltrations?"

"Can't say I've heard that one," Douglas said as he continued tapping on his phone.

"It begins with... but wait, both of you have studied the physics of forced molecular integration, correct?"

"I don't even know what that is," Kevin said with a laugh. "I just started studying *geometry*."

Hearing this, the Autobot revved down, slowing his car form. Douglas looked up from his phone and said, "What is it? What's wrong?"

"We forgot to bring Kevin's homework," Gears said, sounding distressed.

"We can't go back for it now!" Kevin said. "Gears, we have to beat Blowback to Battle Mountain!"

"I suppose you're right," Gears said, accelerating again. "But Optimus Prime and General Marcus will be dismayed if your homework is not finished."

Given how they were not exactly obeying orders by racing off to Battle Mountain, Kevin didn't think incomplete math homework was going to rank all that high on the list of things that would dismay Optimus Prime. But he decided against mentioning that to Gears because he didn't want to give him another reason to reconsider their mission.

"Forced molecular integration," Douglas said, sounding interested. "Is that some kind of technique where you make your enemies take a certain form?"

"Correct, Douglas," Gears said. "So your schooling has included examinations of the underlying quantum physics required for you to understand Dorsata Secundus's technological breakthrough at Polis Station?"

"Not exactly," Douglas said. "You and my father could have some very interesting conversations, though."

"Oh," Gears said. "I will look forward to talking with your father. Meanwhile, I shall endeavor to learn some bedtime stories that will be suitable for young Earth people."

Kevin tried to roll his eyes at Douglas, but he noticed the other boy was tapping faster on his cell phone. Kevin asked, "Any word from your dad?"

"I know he's safe," Douglas said. "Beyond that...I'm guessing he's busy."

"Oh," Kevin said. "I imagine he would be."

Lowering his phone, Douglas looked out the window and snorted. "He's always busy. Hyper-dynamix is everything to him."

"What about your mom?"

"She told my father, 'I'm tired of never seeing my own husband because he's always at work.' So he said, 'I can solve that problem.' They divorced."

"I'm sorry," Kevin said.

"Don't be," Douglas said as he continued gazing out the window. "Despite what my mother said, I think they're both much happier now that they don't have to see each other at all."

No one talked for a few minutes. In the west, the mountains were silhouetted against the night sky. Gears broke the silence. "We could play Twenty Questions."

"Okay, Gears," said Kevin. "But no ancient Cybertronians. It's got to be something or someone from Earth. Or at the very least something or someone *on* Earth."

"Do you want to play, too, Douglas?" Gears asked. "Kevin and I enjoy the game. Do you know it?"

Douglas looked away from the window and faced the nearest speaker from which Gears's voice emanated. "Sure," he said. "My father and I used to play, when I was younger. He said

Twenty Questions was a great introduction to information theory."

"What's that?" Kevin said.

"Think of it as how efficiently you can communicate data, a message, or an idea. What's the minimum information you need to get that data through? Understanding information theory is really important for computing, telecommunications, and a whole lot of other things."

"I get it," Kevin said. "Twenty Questions is kind of like information theory, only in reverse, right? Instead of how efficiently you can communicate an idea, you want to see how quickly you can figure out someone else's idea."

"Exactly," Douglas said. "Whether you win or lose often comes down to asking the right questions, the questions that eliminate the most possibilities. My father used to drill me on those: Is it a unique thing? Is it a class of things? Is it living? Is it a single substance? Does it have parts? Do those parts move? Have I ever seen one? Can I buy one?"

Kevin whistled, impressed. "Those are all great questions. I have to remember those."

"Definitely," Douglas said. "But there's an equally important way to win that has nothing to do with logic. It's social engineering, knowing your opponent and his tendencies. I'd always beat my father that way, and it would drive him crazy."

"What do you mean?"

"I'll demonstrate," Douglas said. "Gears, let's play."

"Very well, Douglas. Kevin and I generally play with the first question being 'Is it animal, vegetable, or mineral?' "

"My father refused to play that way," Douglas said. "He insisted that all questions had to be phrased so they could be answered with a yes or no. But I'm up for doing it your way. All right, then. Gears, is it animal, vegetable, or mineral?"

"Mineral!" Gears said brightly, clearly enjoying having a new opponent.

Douglas glanced at the old chrome radio and smiled slightly. "Is it living?"

"Yes," Gears said. "It is living."

Squeezing two questions into one, Douglas continued, "Is it unique, or is it a member of a class of things?"

"It is unique," Gears said.

"Is it a Cybertronian?"

"It is a Cybertronian."

"Is it aligned with the Autobots or the Decepticons?"

"It is aligned with the Decepticons," Gears said.

"Have I seen it with my own eyes?"

Gears paused. "I do not know."

"My fault, that was a dumb question," Douglas said. "Let me think. Has *Kevin* seen it with his own eyes?"

"Yes," Gears said. "Kevin has seen it with his own eyes."

"Is it Reverb?" Douglas asked.

"Yes, it is Reverb!" Gears said. "You only needed eight questions, Douglas. I am impressed with your skill."

"Social engineering," Douglas told Kevin with a smile. "Gears doesn't have a lot of experience on Earth. You indicated he tends to pick Cybertronians. You introduced the rule that it had to be something on Earth. Put that all together, and there weren't that many choices. Which is how I got to Reverb."

"Clever," Kevin said.

Gears said, "Hmm. I do not think I like being predictable."

Back at the NEST base, Douglas Porter's silver MP3 player lay unnoticed where it had fallen, in the shadows underneath a workstation in the hangar. And when the MP3 player sprouted tiny silver legs from its sides and began to move, none of the technicians, who were hunched over their computer monitors, noticed that, either.

Slowly and silently, the device scooted away from the technicians, keeping to the shadows. It moved into a gap between two computers, then extended its legs to lift its body half an inch higher off the concrete floor. Hairlike silver stalks unspooled from the front of the device, and they began waving in the air. Each stalk was tipped with tiny visual and audio sensors. The stalks swiveled, allowing the device to study its surroundings from every angle. The audio sensors listened intently, cataloging sounds.

To human ears, the hangar's interior would have seemed largely quiet, but the small device picked up every noise. The hum of machinery. Human footsteps in a nearby corridor. A murmur of conversation between two technicians on the far side of the chamber.

The silver intruder was a remote drone, controlled by someone else at another location. It had a mission and raced across the concrete floor like a bug, crossing the open expanse between two rows of computer banks before hiding itself in the shadows along one wall. It proceeded into a long corridor that led deeper into the base. The intruder's visual sensors registered two NEST technicians walking down the corridor ahead. In a split second, the intruder's legs and sensor stalks retracted at the same time that its silver exterior blurred and changed, adjusting to match the color of the dull gray floor.

The soldiers walked by, oblivious to the tiny camouflaged machine that lay motionless a few feet from their boots. The sound of their footsteps had barely faded as the intruder once again extended its legs and sensors. It skittered along the corridor, turned a corner, and stared down the length of another long hallway. At the far end stood a guard. His posture indicated that he was young and bored. Halfway between the intruder and the bored-looking guard, two other soldiers stood in front of a pair of double doors. The two in front of the doors appeared more alert.

The disguised MP3 player moved slowly and silently down the hall, invisible to all but the keenest eye. It crept closer and closer toward the double doors, then picked its way through the narrow space between the first guard's heels and the wall. None of the guards spied the tiny intruder as it slipped through the gap under the doors.

It had entered a laboratory. Four guards stood in the room. Each one carried an unusual black rifle with a broad muzzle, and each wore a backpack that was connected by a hose to a rifle. The backpacks contained liquid carbon fiber, which hardened quickly when sprayed at a target and was capable of immobilizing even a Cybertronian. A NEST technician sat at a desk, typing on a laptop. Beside the laptop was a metal box with a red button on it.

In the center of the room was an iron cage that stood twenty-five feet high. The armed guards faced the cage, making sure to keep their distance by several feet. Inside the cage stood a chrome-armored Cybertronian with gleaming red eyes. He was still and silent, his mechanical arms chained behind his back with three sets of thick, faintly glowing manacles. Another pair of binders encircled his ankles. Lights blinked red on his broad back. The Cybertronian's name was Reverb, and he had been held prisoner at the NEST base since his capture at the Hawthorne Army Depot.

The only sounds in the room were the clicking of the technician's keyboard, the hum of machinery, and the faint whine of Reverb's mechanical systems. Moving with incredible stealth, the little MP3 player crept along one wall until it was halfway between two guards, then slipped very slowly across the floor between them. If either guard had looked down, he might have noticed what resembled a tiny piece of gray concrete moving along the floor, and that might have prompted them to sound an alarm. But neither guard looked down.

The MP3 player arrived beside the cage and recolored itself so it blended in with the cage's bars. After passing between them, it turned gray again to match the floor. When it reached Reverb and began climbing up his massive foot, the color of the chameleon intruder's metal finish shifted to chrome. Then it picked its way up Reverb's leg and side until it reached his shoulder.

Reverb turned his head and his baleful red eyes focused on the disguised MP3 player, which now resembled a tiny chrome chip. Zooming in on the chip, Reverb's mechanical pupils narrowed to a pinprick.

"Hello," the MP3 player squealed in an ultrasonic voice inaudible to humans. "I've come to rescue you."

Reverb pitched his own voice in the same spectrum and said, "Aren't you a little small for a Decepticon?"

"I ain't no Decepticon," the tiny robot squealed. "Human-made, I am, big boy. I swear, you Transformers think you own a patent on robots who can change to look like other things. It's *egotistical* is what it is."

"Humans are insects," Reverb said. "So now we have insects making insects. The universe is an increasingly miserable place."

"Would a little gratitude kill ya?" asked the voice coming from the tiny robot. "I swear, I'd leave you here except I got my orders. Stuff's gonna start happening in a minute. You remember how to work your noisemaker, dontcha?"

The small robot crept down Reverb's neck and vanished beneath his chest plate. Inside his armored breastplate was a cone, the Decepticon's dreaded sonic cannon. The NEST commandos had clamped a sound baffle onto it and added an electronic lock that prevented Reverb from activating his primary weapon.

Tiny tools extended from the metal chip of the small robot's body and began picking at the baffle. The lights on Reverb's back turned yellow. "That tickles," grumbled Reverb, shifting slightly inside the cage.

The technician noticed Reverb's movement. He looked up, saw that Reverb was still secured by the chains and electronic restraints, and then returned his attention to his monitor.

Burrowing under Reverb's armor, the tiny robot moved around the edges of the sonic cannon, cut the electronic lock's power connection, and then skittered onto the sound baffle itself. It extended a miniature saw and began cutting through the attachments that held the baffle in place. A moment later, the attachments were severed.

The lights on Reverb's back turned green. The guard who had the clearest view of Reverb's back blinked at that moment, and when he saw the green lights, he reached up with one hand to rub his eyes. He'd been standing watch for so long that he thought he was imagining things.

"Showtime," the MP3 player's voice said. "Give 'em a shout."

A loud whine sounded from inside the cage. The NEST tech looked away from his monitor and saw that Reverb had opened his armored chest plate, revealing the cannon capped with its sound baffle. The tech said, "That's a lovely toy you've got there, Reverb. Too bad for you that we turned it off."

The baffle fell away from the cannon and landed on the concrete floor with a loud clank.

Reverb's mouth and jaw mechanisms twisted into a nasty grin.

The technician reached for the red button, but before his finger got there, an enormous blast of sound ripped out from Reverb's chest. The tech flew backward, and his workstation and laptop tumbled after him. He hit the concrete and lay still. The two guards in front of the cage were sprawled on the concrete as well, their hands clapped over their ears.

Behind Reverb, the other two guards hadn't been hit by the full impact of the cannon, but the sound blast had temporarily deafened them. They couldn't hear their own shouts as they yelled into their headsets, calling for backup.

Then one guard fell, jerking spasmodically as he hit the floor. The remaining guard looked at his fallen colleague in puzzlement, just in time to see a small square of concrete race across the floor and start climbing his own boot. He felt sharp little legs poking into him through his uniform, and then came a sharper poke, followed by a massive jolt of electricity that coursed through his body. The last guard dropped his weapon and collapsed beside it.

The tiny robot crowed, "Now that's what I'd call a shocking development!"

"Stop chattering and free me," Reverb said. "Now!"

It scurried over to the controls for Reverb's restraints. The small robot had just managed to free Reverb's legs and had shut down power to the manacles when the room's double doors burst inward and six soldiers wearing protective sound-damping headgear raced in, carrying machine guns. Seeing Reverb, the soldiers opened fire, the bullets striking sparks off his armor.

Reverb's sonic cannon was still recharging. Although the small robot had cut power to the manacles, the chains did not automatically fall away from Reverb's wrists. Reverb grunted angrily as the bullets whizzed through the surrounding cage's bars and pinged off his chest plate. Using an optical readout to check the status of his sonic cannon again, he saw that the cannon still required twenty more seconds for a full recharge. He also calculated that if he fired now, he wouldn't incapacitate the new arrivals, but the concussive force would be enough to drive them backward despite their ear protection.

"Guess we gotta do this the hard way," Reverb growled. He hunched his shoulders, straining against his chains with such force that he broke free, shattering the restraints. He interlocked his fingers and swung at the cage's door, and it snapped free of its hinges. The soldiers intensified their fire, but Reverb shoved his bulk through the cage's broken doorway and swatted the soldiers aside.

Reverb burst through the doors and out into the corridor. The tiny robot followed and skittered up the Decepticon's leg as he stomped down the hallway. Reverb's sonic cannon was now fully charged, and he blasted open the doors.

The force of the sonic blast also took out the surrounding frame and walls. Reverb moved through the hole he had created and entered the hangar, where he found technicians scrambling away from their stations and radar screens. But the soldiers inside the hangar didn't run. Seeing Reverb, they opened fire with their machine guns and raked him with bullets.

A squad of NEST commandos ran from the other side of the hangar. These commandos were armed with carbon-fiber sprayers. Reverb fired at them. A noise like a thunderclap shattered the radar screens and knocked the commandos head over heels. Reverb scanned the hangar for any sign of Autobots, hoping he might have the chance to shred some metal. He was especially eager to carve up Gears, whom he held almost entirely responsible for capturing him. But everywhere he looked, he only saw the humans whom he regarded as little more than annoying insects, stinging him with their primitive weapons.

Reverb kicked a heavy table across the hangar, launching it at two commandos who had made the mistake of struggling to their feet. As the commandos dived away from the table, the tiny robot tapped Reverb and said, "Fun time is over. This jailbreak ain't no freebie, you know. Boss man's got orders for you."

"Who's the boss man?" Reverb snarled.

"That's on a need-to-know basis," the voice said, "and you don't need to know. But he's got some info you might want. Like where to find another one of those Cybertronian storehouses you were looking for. And guess what? Your old friend Gears will be there."

"*Now* you're talking," Reverb said as he fired a burst at a row of large monitors. "I've got a score to settle with that junk heap." He strode across the hangar, walking past wounded soldiers, and ripped the entry doors apart. Carrying the tiny robot with him, he leaped out into the darkness. Overhead, stars twinkled in the chilly night sky. Gears lumbered toward a parking lot. "Which way to the storehouse and Gears?"

The small voice said, "Transmitting data."

"Got it." Reverb grunted as a stream of data flowed into his brain. He was about to read through the data when his eyes swept the insects' vehicles in the parking lot, and his attention fell upon a black jeep with gleaming rims. Although he had never seen the vehicle before, he realized it belonged to one of the guards who had been stationed outside his cage. To Reverb's irritation, the guard had talked for hours about his jeep and how he'd saved up to install a custom sound system that included a powerful subwoofer that made other drivers feel his music's bass vibrations before they saw him coming. A "boomin' system," the young braggart had called it.

Reverb decided the jeep was just what he

needed. He scanned the vehicle, analyzing, measuring, and digitally memorizing every feature. When he was done with his scan, Reverb decided to leave a present for the guard who was so obviously in love with his jeep and its precious sound system. Reverb lifted one foot and brought it down hard on the jeep's hood. He proceeded to stomp on the vehicle until it was reduced to a crushed mound of metal and broken glass.

When Reverb was done, the tiny robot said impatiently, "I don't suppose you have any interest in the data I sent you?"

"Right, the data," Reverb said as he sifted through the downloaded information. "Battle Mountain, eh? Never heard of the place." As he assumed the form of an immaculate black jeep with gleaming rims, he adjusted the volume on his even more powerful adaptation of the demolished vehicle's custom sound system, and his voice thundered, "But before the night is over, everyone at Battle Mountain will have heard of me."

The small robot, now affixed to the jeep's glove compartment, said, "We'll get there sooner if you stop talking and—"

Its words were lost as Reverb burned rubber and roared off into the night.

Chapter Eleven

NIGHT JOURNEY

Still disguised as a vintage British sports car and carrying Kevin and Douglas, Gears sped down a dark highway. A few miles ahead of him was Bumblebee, speeding along in his own form as a yellow-and-black sports car. On their journey so far, the two Autobots had encountered little traffic.

Gears and the two boys had played several games of Twenty Questions, with Douglas coaching Kevin on how to outthink his opponent.

Now, the older boy was staring out the window into the night, apparently lost in his own thoughts except when he tapped a message on his expensive cell phone.

Kevin was anxious about his brother and the possibility that he might be trapped in the Cybertronian storehouse near Battle Mountain. It was weird to be with Douglas, too. He hadn't mentioned Charlene at all—Kevin wondered if they had broken up. He thought it best not to ask just in case. Thinking of Charlene made him think of Gilbert. He missed Gilbert. But thinking about his best friend made him sad, so Kevin tried to empty his mind.

He was also exhausted, and despite his best efforts to stay awake, Kevin felt his chin dip again and again, his eyelids growing heavy. And before he knew it, he was asleep.

But not for long. He jerked awake, and for a

moment he had no idea where he was or what he was doing in a strange car in the middle of the night with Douglas Porter, of all people. Then he remembered, and he rubbed his eyes, yawning.

"You are awake, Kevin," Gears said through the radio. "I hope you are at least partially recharged."

"I'm okay," Kevin said. "But I'm starving."

"So am I," Douglas said.

"I forgot that you need food as well as sleep," Gears said, sounding disappointed in himself. "We should stop."

Douglas looked up from his phone. "There's a burger joint with a drive-through in Tonopah. It's only a few minutes out of our way."

"My brother may not have a few extra minutes," Kevin said. "Forget I mentioned food."

"You're right," Douglas added. "You can bet Blowback's not stopping for burgers."

Gears said, "We are headed into a dangerous situation. You two need to be fueled. I have a communications channel open with Bumblebee. I will ask for his input."

The car continued driving itself along the dark highway while Kevin and Douglas waited. An eighth of a mile later, Gears said, "Bumblebee is far enough ahead of us that he can obtain food and then wait for us at the turnoff to State Route 376. We should not be delayed by more than a few seconds."

"That's great!" Douglas said. "Tell Bumblebee I want two bison burgers on whole wheat buns with Gruyère cheese, Vidalia onions, baby spinach, Dijon mustard, and a bottle of mineral water."

Kevin said, "Can I just get two cheeseburgers with fries and a root beer?"

Gears relayed the boys' orders to Bumblebee.

When he was done, he said, "Bumblebee said Kevin's order will take less time. He will order four cheeseburgers, two large orders of fries, and two root beers."

Douglas sighed. "So much for robots obeying humans."

Kevin said, "I just thought of something, Gears. How is Bumblebee going to pay for the food?"

"I am not certain," Gears admitted. "I shall ask him." Several seconds later, Gears said, "Bumblebee says payment will not be a problem. He has access to a database of NEST credit-card numbers."

"Oh," Kevin said. "Is he authorized to access those numbers? I mean, is that...legal?"

"I don't know," Gears said.

Douglas said, "Just tell Bumblebee to be careful about which number he uses. We're already in for an earful from General Marcus."

"I will tell Bumblebee to be careful," Gears said. "It is my understanding that when he is on a mission, he sometimes forgets certain rules, and he can be a bit...dramatic."

On the outskirts of Tonopah, Nevada, eighteen-year-old Jimmy Lemmon was helming the drive-through window at the Kwiki-Burger when he heard a voice call over the drive-through inter-com, *"Howdy, partner!"* The voice, which sounded like something from an old TV show, slipped into a weird singsong tone and pro-ceeded to order four cheeseburgers, two large fries, and two root beers.

Jimmy Lemmon placed the order, then said, "Cash or credit?"

The unseen customer sang in response, "*I don't have the time to waste. Charge it!*"

Jimmy eyed a monitor and saw the customer's credit card had been approved for payment. He turned to his assistant, who handed him a large paper bag that contained the customer's order. Jimmy turned back to the window just as a yellow-and-black car pulled up to the pickup window. The driver's window descended. Jimmy could not help noticing that the car was empty.

Jimmy peered into the car, then craned his head out of the drive-through window to look around. He knew the empty car had to be a prank and told himself to be cool. He didn't mind appearing on some friend's Internet video, but he did mind looking like an idiot scratching his head at the sight of an apparently magical car. But except for the sports car, the drive-through lane was empty, and none of Jimmy's friends emerged from the Kwiki-Burger's manicured shrubs, laughing from behind a cell phone camera.

The car revved its engine, then its radio came to life and the old TV voice demanded, *"Hand it over, partner!"*

Spooked and no longer caring about being laughed at on the Internet, Jimmy leaned out the drive-through window as far as he could and let the bag of food drop neatly on the empty driver's seat.

"Thank yuh, thank yuh very much," drawled the empty car, accompanied by recorded applause. And then, as Jimmy wriggled back into the drive-through booth, the car peeled out and vanished into the Nevada night. For the rest of his life, Jimmy Lemmon would tell

the tale of the ghostly car, and he would swear it was absolutely true.

Three minutes later, Bumblebee was back on the highway when Gears pulled up alongside him. Neither car slowed as each lowered a facing window, and then a robotic arm within the yellow car lifted the bag of food and extended it into the silver one.

At the Hyperdynamix complex, the Autobots still had not found the three Decepticons who had infiltrated the facility, leaving General Marcus almost as frustrated as Ironhide. Likewise, Dr. Alexander Porter had grown increasingly anxious and irate with every passing minute that he remained hidden in his corporate vault. Marcus was almost relieved when an aide told him a commando from NEST's Rapid Response Base needed to speak with him.

Marcus took the phone, listened, then bellowed, "What?!" On the other end of the line, the NEST commando began to dutifully repeat what he'd just said before Marcus interrupted, "No, no, I heard you the first time, son. Hold on." Marcus lifted his gaze to Optimus Prime and said, "Reverb has escaped."

"How?"

"He managed to break his restraints and blast his way out of his cage, doing substantial damage to the base. He was last seen heading north."

"Casualties?" said Optimus.

"No, but over a dozen men were injured."

"What happened to Bumblebee and Gears?"

General Marcus relayed the question to the base. A few seconds later, his face went red. He looked back to Optimus and said, "They left the base almost ninety minutes before Reverb escaped. Kevin Bowman was with them, and also Douglas Porter."

Optimus said, "I think I know where they're headed."

"I think I do, too," Marcus said. "Battle Mountain."

Optimus nodded and activated his own communications system. "Ironhide, return to the staging area. Ratchet and I will continue the hunt for the intruders. We need you at Battle Mountain as soon as possible."

"Right away, boss," Ironhide said. "I was getting tired of playing hide-and-seek."

Chapter Twelve
BATTLE MOUNTAIN

According to local lore, the town of Battle Mountain was founded in 1870, about the same time that the Central Pacific Railroad reached the area, and got its name from a conflict in 1850 between white settlers and Shoshone Indians in the mountain range to the southwest of the town. The Central Pacific Railroad had long since become part of the Union Pacific, and the Union Pacific westbound track still went through the middle of the town. For more than 140 years, Battle Mountain was known for its gold-mining operations, and most people considered it a peaceful, quiet place.

Gears was nearing Battle Mountain when he directed his headlights to focus on Bumblebee by the side of the road up ahead. Bumblebee had assumed his bipedal form, and he stood with his one thumb jokingly lifted up into the air as if he were pretending to hitchhike. Gears slowed to a stop beside Bumblebee, and then the sleek silver car began to clatter and buck, rising as Gears reconfigured his parts into his normal form. Kevin and Douglas gasped as the car's doors flipped open and Gears eased them out of their seats, placing the boys gently on the ground next to Bumblebee.

From where they stood, they could see moving

headlights that marked the interstate in the distance, just beyond the lights of the town of Battle Mountain. Bumblebee pointed to a dirt road that led up into the dark hills as he broadcast an old song that proclaimed that this must be his destination.

"My internal map agrees," Gears said. "That should be Antler Peak."

"So let's get moving," Kevin said as he started walking toward the dirt road. He'd only taken a few steps when a loud whistle pierced the air and a missile slammed into the ground ahead of him. The explosion threw Kevin onto his back and showered dirt all over him, Douglas, and the two Autobots.

Gears activated his infrared scanners as he rapidly reconfigured his arms into cannons. He saw a black-armored Cybertronian marching up the highway toward them. One of his forearms ended in a gleaming double-bladed ax, and his eyes burned red in the darkness, leaving little doubt that he was a Decepticon.

"Blowback, I presume," muttered Gears. He extended one arm in front of Kevin and Douglas and said, "Stay here. Go hide behind those rocks, and *do not* move until we come back for you."

Bumblebee cycled through his own weapons as he strode over to stand beside Gears. Leaving the boys behind, the two Autobots marched down the highway. They came to a halt about a hundred yards away from the Decepticon.

"Autobots," Blowback said just loudly enough to be heard across the distance. "Once you were gods. Now you're chauffeurs and errand boys for insects."

"We seek peace," Gears said. "And in doing so, we conduct ourselves with honor. Surrender and you will not be harmed."

"Surrender?" Blowback laughed, a harsh, grating sound. "I'll leave both of you to bleach in the desert sun!" The blades of Blowback's ax began to turn, slowly at first, then faster and faster, until his weapon became a blur.

Bumblebee fired up a recording that declared he was ready to rumble. He raised his plasma cannon and fired at Blowback's head. The Decepticon jerked his upper body to the side and rushed forward as the bolts sailed past him.

Blowback moved quickly, swinging the ax toward the back of Bumblebee's neck. Bumblebee ducked, and the ax whizzed over his head. Gears charged at Blowback's unprotected rear, but Blowback brought his arm around in a full circle, nearly decapitating Gears. The Autobot could feel the rush of air produced by the whirling ax blades as he stumbled backward, falling to one knee.

Bumblebee lowered his shoulder and drove it into Blowback's side before the Decepticon could take advantage of Gears's downed position. Blowback shuffled backward and stopped, his mouth twisted into a terrible metal grin as his spinning ax blades struck the pavement and sent sparks flying.

"Come on, if you dare!" Blowback taunted. Then he turned and ran for the town of Battle Mountain. Bumblebee and Gears raced after him.

Still crouching behind the rocks where the Autobots had left them, Kevin and Douglas peered around and watched the three hulking robots grow smaller as they ran off. The robots continued to exchange fire, but soon the sound of their battle began to fade, and then the boys lost sight of them.

Kevin shivered in the night air and zipped up his sweatshirt before he started walking, skirting the crater left by Blowback's missile as he moved forward onto the dirt road that led into the hills. Without looking back at Douglas, he said, "Don't tell me we should wait."

"No argument from me," Douglas said as he walked quickly to catch up with Kevin. "We'd just get in the way if we tried to help Bumblebee and Gears fight Blowback. Better that we try to find the storehouse."

"If we find it," Kevin said, "and I'm able to get inside, I'm not waiting for Gears and Bumblebee. I'm just going in."

"Kevin, enough!" Douglas said with a laugh. "I *agree* with you, all right? We'll find the storehouse, and we'll go in together." Douglas activated his cell phone, its white light illuminating his handsome face. "According to the data I have, the site should be up there and to the right."

"Above the old gold mine."

"X marks the spot," Douglas said. "Just like a treasure map."

"I don't care if that storehouse is full of diamonds," Kevin said as he looked at the dark silhouettes of the surrounding hills. "I just want my brother back."

To Gears's annoyance, his left leg still wasn't working quite right, leaving him struggling to keep up with Bumblebee. And he kept having to dodge missiles and fire from Blowback, who remained ahead of them as he led them toward the lighted strip that was Interstate 80.

Gears wasn't happy that Blowback was heading for the town of Battle Mountain. Humans were fragile creatures, and if they wound up in the middle of a fight between Cybertronians, they would certainly suffer. He hoped Blowback would make his stand before they reached the town, or that Bumblebee would catch Blowback, or that Battle Mountain's inhabitants would be smart enough to stay in their homes, out of sight and out of danger.

Ahead of Gears, Bumblebee and Blowback kept peppering each other with fire from their cannons, but neither scored a full direct hit. Blowback reached the highway first, and one of his feet crushed a length of chain-link fence.

Tires squealed and horns honked as drivers saw one giant robot chase another across the highway. Hurrying after Bumblebee and Blowback, Gears jumped over the ruined fence and then bounded over the eastbound highway lanes, dodging cars until he landed in the dusty median. Gears looked to an overpass and saw a Nevada Highway Patrol cruiser. Behind the cruiser's wheel, the officer's mouth fell open as he gazed back at Gears.

Facing the cruiser, Gears increased his voice's volume as he said, "Remain in your vehicle, officer. We will handle this." The wide-eyed police officer managed to nod as Gears hurdled the westbound lanes of Interstate 80 and proceeded after Bumblebee and Blowback.

Blowback arrived at the edge of a construction site, where a row of blue plastic portable toilets was lined up beside a concrete wall. The

Decepticon glanced back, saw Bumblebee and Gears in pursuit, and launched a fusillade from his cannon. The shots sailed wide of Bumblebee, knocking down a utility pole that sent broken power lines snaking and sparking into the street. Gears fired a missile of his own, but Blowback dodged them by leaping past the portable toilets. The missile arced into the toilets, sending sheets of melted plastic and sprays of blue disinfectant skyward.

Blowback ran up a street, came to a halt at a T intersection, and turned to confront his yellow-and-black opponent. Bumblebee slammed into Blowback, and the two Cybertronians locked arms, their pistons grinding and motors shrieking as each tried to knock the other off his feet.

Gears arrived at the T intersection, saw the grappling Transformers, and quickly surveyed the area Blowback had chosen as a battleground. To his left, Gears saw a deli and a dilapidated motel. To the right lay another motel and two casinos. On the other side of the street, across the intersection, were train tracks where some empty freight cars were resting. Gears hoped he and Bumblebee would be able to push Blowback across the street, away from the motels, and from the people inside them.

Blowback broke free from Bumblebee, shoved him back, and swung his ax hard, clipping the Autobot and bringing down another utility pole. The surrounding streetlights went dark as the pole crashed and bounced against the ground. Bumblebee whirled and fired blindly, launching a missile that sent a motel sign spinning off its moorings in a bright blossom of fire.

As the explosion swelled and illuminated the

area, Gears saw movement just beyond the line of freight cars. When he saw what was moving, he suddenly realized why Blowback had run to the town of Battle Mountain instead of to the location of the ancient Cybertronian storehouse.

"Bumblebee, look out!" Gears shouted as three more Decepticons lumbered toward the train tracks.

Kevin and Douglas followed the dirt road until it ended at the abandoned mine. An ugly slash hacked out of the hillside, the mine was surrounded by broken machinery and old trash. Seeing the mine's entrance, which gaped like a wide mouth, Kevin shivered and said, "It looks hungry."

Douglas consulted his cell phone, then pocketed it as he began climbing up the scrubby hillside to the left of the mine's entrance. "The storehouse should be this way," Douglas said. "Come on."

Kevin followed. They climbed until they reached a shelf of level ground. Douglas pointed to the next rise, a couple of hundred feet above their position, and said, "We have to get up there."

"Doesn't look like a terribly difficult climb."

Douglas glanced back at the lights of Battle Mountain below them and gasped. "Oh, no. Look!"

Kevin followed Douglas's gaze and saw a bright orange flash of light against the darkness. The boys were too far away to make out any details around the area of the explosion, but Kevin said, "I guess Gears and Bee caught up with that Decepticon. I hope they're okay."

"It's two against one," Douglas said. "The

Autobots will be fine. Now, let's go find that storehouse."

They kept climbing but were distracted by more explosions from the battle below. A few seconds after each bright burst of light, the cracking booms of the distant explosions reached their ears. Despite his concern for the Autobots, as well as the people of Battle Mountain, Kevin had faith in Gears and Bumblebee, and he trusted them to do whatever was necessary to stop Blowback.

Kevin scrambled up after Douglas to a flat shelf below a sloping wall, a slab of rock about seventy feet shy of the top of the hill. Douglas examined the wall and said, "This is it."

The wall was some fifty feet across, broken by outcroppings of rock, stubborn bushes, and small crevasses. If Kevin hadn't known better, he never would have suspected the aged, weathered wall wasn't a product of normal erosion. He said, "Look for an entrance."

Douglas eyed the wide wall. "Uh, does the entrance to an ancient Cybertronian weapons storehouse look like anything in particular?"

Kevin thought. "At Hawthorne, the entrance had some kind of mechanism in a hollow on the wall. Gears was the one who actually opened the thing." Kevin ran his hands over the rock's surface and peered doubtfully into the first crack he found. "I hope there aren't scorpions or spiders in there."

"Or snakes," Douglas added.

"A lot of help you are!"

Douglas laughed as he pulled his cell phone out of his pocket and activated it. "Use your phone, Kevin. Shine it into the crevasses."

"Oh, yeah," Kevin said. "I should have thought of that." He pulled out his own phone and switched it on. "I'll start on this side, you start over there, and we'll meet in the middle."

Moving their hands over the wall, the boys found several crevasses, but when they directed the lights from their respective cell phones into gaps, they saw all were shallow or empty. Kevin worked his way slowly across the rock face, trying not to imagine his brother and the other soldiers starving somewhere inside their stone prison. He said, "Douglas, what if there's a crevasse but it's too high for us to reach?"

"Then we'll wait for a Cybertronian to get here and give us a boost," Douglas said. "Seriously, Kevin, we can only do what we can. Don't drive yourself crazy thinking about anything beyond that."

They kept searching, trying to ignore the muffled thumps and thuds from the town below. Kevin nearly jumped from fright when he heard

Douglas whistle. Kevin said, "What is it? Did you find something?"

"Yes," Douglas said gravely. "Yes, I think I did."

"Let me see!"

Kevin hurried over and found Douglas looking up at a gap in the rock about six feet above the shelf. Douglas shined his cell phone into the crevasse, and Kevin could just make out a large, dull black handle. Douglas said, "Looks like a metal lever. Did you see how Gears held or turned the thing?"

"No," Kevin said. "He just reached up into the wall, and then the wall opened."

Douglas stepped away from the wall and stooped down to grab a large, loose stone. As he hefted the stone back to the wall, he said, "Help me gather stones. We'll stack them up, and I'll climb them to reach the handle."

The two boys grunted as they shoved loose rocks across the shelf, creating a pile of stones for Douglas to stand on. He clambered up, testing his balance, and reached into the hole.

Kevin said, "Can you reach the lever?"

A moment later, Douglas said, "Yeah, I've got it. I don't know whether to turn it or pull or push or what, though. I'm not sure if I'll even be able to budge the thing." Douglas pushed hard. Nothing happened. He shifted his arm to readjust his grip. "Whoa."

"Whoa?" Kevin said, his eyes wide with anticipation. "Whoa, what?"

"It's moving. Pretty easily, too."

A grinding noise sounded from somewhere inside the rocky hill. As the two boys watched, a crack appeared about twenty feet above the shelf, widening into a horizontal line. Vertical lines appeared in the stone, stretching down to the shelf. With a low groan, the wide slab of rock began to descend into the ground. The boys stepped back as dirt and small stones bounced away from the slab.

The groaning noise ceased as the slab came to a stop, and the boys faced a large, yawning passage, an entrance that led directly into the mountain. A dim yellow light illuminated the passage's walls, which appeared remarkably smooth.

"Duane!" Kevin yelled. He rushed into the passage before Douglas could stop him.

Chapter Thirteen
VOICES IN THE DARK

Bumblebee was trying to divert Blowback away from the Battle Mountain motels when Gears saw the three approaching Decepticons smash through the freight cars on the tracks. Gears rushed closer to Bumblebee and shouted, "Bumblebee! Back to back!"

Keeping his eyes on Blowback, Bumblebee shifted his feet and leaped to land behind Gears while Gears watched the other three Decepticons. Gears said, "Now we can't be surrounded."

Blowback laughed. "I like these odds better!" Gesturing to the other Decepticons, he continued. "Meet my associates...Sawtooth, Burnrate, and Roadrash. If that's too hard for you to remember, just call them your executioners!"

Sawtooth was a rusty-looking robot with spikes up and down his arms and back. Burnrate had large flamethrowers mounted on his forearms. Roadrash's armor plating was an ugly mottled gray and red. All of them looked eager to tear into the Autobots.

Ignoring Blowback, Gears faced the deadly trio of Decepticons and said, "I suggest you retreat or surrender. Optimus Prime and Ironhide are just minutes behind us. If they catch you here, this town will be your grave."

"Optimus Prime?" Sawtooth said, a nervous quaver in his voice.

"He's bluffing, you fool!" Blowback roared. "Take them! Take them now!"

Although Gears was still not fully recovered from his near-fatal encounter with Reverb, he had trained extensively with the other Autobots at the NEST base in the past month. The old weapons specialist, Ironhide, had been a tough taskmaster, insisting that Gears learn tactics for everything from covering fire to hand-to-hand combat, and also the importance of teamwork. According to Ironhide, when a soldier was outnumbered, the soldier should use his attackers' numbers against them and seize any opportunities that presented themselves.

Now, with his back up against Bumblebee's, Gears was glad Ironhide had been such a demanding teacher. Gears said, "Stay with me, Bumblebee."

Bumblebee automatically matched Gears's movements to stick close to him as Gears ducked and rolled and fired a barrage of plasma at the feet of Roadrash, who yelped and jumped aside as Gears and Bumblebee barreled through the space he'd occupied, then whirled, cannons blazing. And just as Gears had anticipated, Roadrash landed in front of Sawtooth, who in turn stepped into Burnrate's line of fire.

"Look out!" yelled Burnrate, but he had already ignited his flame jets, unleashing a blast of fire that washed over Sawtooth's back. The spiked Decepticon howled in pain, then plowed into Roadrash in his haste to escape the intense heat.

As Sawtooth stumbled, Gears unloaded his plasma cannons into the Decepticon's armored torso, driving him to his knees. Bumblebee fired his own cannon at Blowback, forcing him to duck.

"Spread out!" Blowback yelled. "Don't get in each other's way!"

Gears kicked Sawtooth in the face, knocking him backward onto the street. Unfortunately, Bumblebee had taken his eyes off Roadrash, who unfurled a long chain with a spiked ball at the end. The ball bashed Bumblebee in the back of the head, sending him stumbling over Sawtooth's prone form.

Bumblebee recovered his balance and stomped on Sawtooth before throwing himself between Gears and their attackers. Roadrash raced forward and swung his chain, forcing Bumblebee to duck. The spiked ball whipped over Bumblebee's crouched form, and Gears reached out with lightning speed to grab the ball's chain.

Gears pulled hard and fast, yanking Roadrash toward him as Sawtooth grabbed Bumblebee's ankles and sent him sprawling.

With Roadrash still off-balance, Gears took a firmer grip on the chain, whirling around the hapless Decepticon in a stumbling arc. Then Gears let go, and Roadrash flew straight toward a casino's red-and-white marquee, crashing through the sign in a shower of sparks and bashing a large hole in the front of the building. Gears saw frightened people running quickly out of the building's side doors.

He turned to see Bumblebee on the ground grappling with Sawtooth and Burnrate. Each of the Decepticons had grabbed an arm as Blowback raised his missile launcher, taking aim at Bumblebee's unprotected torso.

Gears fired his cannon. The road in front of

Blowback exploded, spraying asphalt and gravel everywhere and causing the Decepticon to stumble backward. Blowback fired a missile, which missed Bumblebee and streaked toward Gears instead. Gears flung himself on the ground as the missile tore past his head, the intense heat raising blisters in the silver paint on his shoulder armor. The missile's flight ended when it struck Roadrash, and the explosion that followed blew out the casino's windows as well as those in the buildings up and down the street.

The explosion also sent coins, dice, and brightly colored chips flying out of the shattered casino. The debris pinged off the robots' armor. As burnt bits of playing cards fluttered down through the air, Gears risked a glance behind him and saw Roadrash sink to his knees, a massive hole blown completely through his smoking armor. The red sparks of his eyes flickered and died.

Bumblebee kicked free from Burnrate and sprang backward to stand beside Gears as the casino continued to burn behind them. Burnrate and Sawtooth picked themselves up and stood on either side of Blowback, who no longer looked so confident.

Gears muttered, "The odds are looking more in our favor, Bumblebee. Let's finish this and get back to the boys."

Inside the mountain, Kevin ran through the smooth-walled corridor until he arrived at another corridor that stretched out to his left and right. On the wall in front of him, he found what appeared to be a circular flat-screen monitor embedded above a triangular grille. The monitor glowed dimly.

As Kevin looked at the monitor, whorls of white static appeared on the screen. A few seconds later, the static disappeared. Kevin wondered if he'd triggered an alarm.

"Duane!" Kevin yelled. Although he had no idea where he was going, he turned and rushed down the corridor to his left, holding his phone out in front of him for illumination.

The corridor emptied into a round chamber similar to the one Kevin and Gears had discovered at Hawthorne. As his phone's light played out across the chamber, Kevin was not entirely surprised to see ancient Cybertronian cannons and other unidentifiable technology. But unlike the artifacts he'd seen at Hawthorne, the cannons and technology in this chamber were dull and rusted. Kevin cautiously extended the toe of his sneaker to tap the muzzle of a cannon. The physical contact produced a brittle cracking sound, and most of the muzzle crumbled and fell away into a small pile of dust.

Footsteps sounded from behind Kevin, and then Douglas arrived, breathing hard. Douglas gasped. "What'd you find?"

"Junk," Kevin said. "It's all junk."

Douglas increased the intensity of his own cell phone's light and directed its beam across the ceiling. The stone was marred by a dark discoloration. Douglas said, "It looks like there was a leak here. Maybe from a natural spring or from centuries of rainwater seeping in. Must've flooded the place and ruined everything ages ago. I hope that didn't happen down the other corridor."

The other corridor. Kevin had been so overwhelmed by the sight of the useless Cybertronian relics that he had momentarily forgotten about the corridor that he'd bypassed. He pushed past Douglas and ran out of the chamber, heading back the way he'd come.

Kevin ran past the intersection that led back outside and continued into the right-hand corridor. In the darkness up ahead, he saw a small pinpoint of red light blinking on and off. He was almost breathless when he arrived at the end of the corridor, where he discovered the red light was embedded on the surface of a large metal door. The light blinked steadily. The door showed no signs of rust.

Kevin hammered on the door. "Duane! Duane!" He heard only the echo of his own voice. He was about to call out again when he heard an odd sound, a deep electronic tone that came from behind him. He realized the sound was a Cybertronian voice.

Kevin spun around quickly, expecting to see a robot standing right behind him. Instead, he gazed down the length of the corridor and saw the white rectangle of Douglas's cell phone.

"Kevin!" Douglas shouted. "This old monitor...It's talking!"

Intending to head back to Douglas's position, Kevin took a step away from the door when a loud, inhuman voice echoed, "*Kevin, thissoldMONitoritssss...TALK-KING.*" The harsh, grinding voice dissolved into static, then went silent.

Kevin ran back to Douglas, who was staring at the circular monitor over the triangular grille. Kevin said, "What'd you do?"

"Nothing," Douglas said. "I didn't touch the thing."

"Well, there's a door at the end of the corridor, and it's locked. We have to figure out how to open it."

And then the inhuman voice spoke again, its tone steadier as it said, *"Can you COMmunicate using this dialect?"*

Facing the glowing white screen, Douglas said, "We understand you. How do you know how to speak English?"

"This facility periodically scans available COM-munications frequencies. Electronic transmissions are analyzed in preparation for contact scenarios with indigenous life. Are you indigenous life?"

"Yes," Douglas said. "We're humans." He glanced at Kevin, then continued. "We have formed an alliance with the Cybertronians on this world. Are you a form of Cybertronian?"

"*I am an artificial intelligence with the authority to maintain and defend this facility.*"

"And you have done a superb job," Douglas said. "We are very grateful."

"*Your gratitude is of no importance,*" the voice said coolly. "*State your purpose here.*"

"As allies of your people," Douglas said, "we need access to the locked chamber inside this storehouse."

"*Your purpose here is accepted.*"

Douglas smiled smugly at Kevin and said, "Well, that was easy enough."

"*Provide the authorization code for access.*"

Douglas stopped smiling. "The code. Yes, the code. The code was lost thousands of years ago. But I can assure you that it's all right to unlock the chamber at the end of this corridor and let us in."

"*Your assurance is meaningless. Provide the authorization code for access.*"

Kevin stepped closer to the monitor. Speaking into the grille, he said, "We'll get the code soon. But first we need to know what's in that chamber."

"*Information about that portion of my inventory is restricted without the authorization code. Or, as a backup, provide identification of the restricted item or items. Such an identification will indicate that access should be granted.*"

Douglas said, "Does that mean you *can* tell us about the rest of your inventory?"

"*Nonrestricted information is available.*"

"Okay," Douglas said. "Please list the nonrestricted items in your inventory."

The computer began speaking in the Cybertronian language, uttering words that meant nothing to Kevin or Douglas. The computer's monotonous voice had been speaking for almost forty-five seconds when Douglas interrupted. "All that stuff turned to rust thousands of years ago. What information can't you reveal?"

"*Identification of the restricted portion of my inventory.*"

"The restricted portion of your inventory is what's behind that locked door?"

"*Correct.*"

"Can you answer other questions pertaining to the restricted portion of your inventory?"

"*Nonrestricted information is available.*"

Smiling broadly at Kevin, Douglas said, "So it's Twenty Questions all over again."

"*Twenty questions is incorrect. After twelve inquiries concerning the restricted portion of my inventory, access will no longer be granted, and this facility will enter lockdown mode.*"

"Sure, *Twelve* Questions," Douglas said, still smiling. "That's what I meant. Okay, so my first question is —"

"*You have already asked two questions concerning the restricted portion of my inventory. I am waiting for your third question.*"

Douglas stopped smiling. "Of course. Ten questions left. Give me a moment."

Chapter Fourteen
ANCIENT SECRETS

Blowback, Sawtooth, and Burnrate advanced slowly on Gears and Bumblebee, trying to back them into the burning casino. Gears yelled, "Break left!" as he shoved Bumblebee in that direction.

The two Autobots bolted past Sawtooth, the impact of their heavy feet causing parked cars to bounce on their shock absorbers before the Autobots stopped and turned to face their pursuers. Gears noticed humans streaming out of the motels in their sleepwear. Some people were carrying children or luggage, and they appeared to be trying to run away as quickly as possible. But others were lingering outside the buildings as they aimed cell phones and cameras at the robots fighting in the sleepy mining town.

Pausing behind Bumblebee, Gears looked at the gawkers and yelled, "Go! Run!"

Blowback realized Gears was more focused on the humans than on his own safety, and he saw an opening for an attack. Blowback darted around Sawtooth, swung his spinning ax, and clouted Gears in the side, sending him flying into the motel. The motel shook on its foundation. The remaining gawkers fled.

Blowback was about to strike Gears again when Bumblebee fired his cannons, scoring hits on Blowback's midsection. Blowback staggered backward, grabbing at his side. He almost toppled, but Sawtooth caught him, at the same time firing at Bumblebee.

Gears and Bumblebee fell back, with the three Decepticons following. Bumblebee nudged Gears to get his attention, and then Bumblebee jutted his chin to the left, where most of the freight train remained on the tracks. Gears nodded, and the two sprang to the left, leaping over the train cars as the Decepticons launched missiles.

Gears said, "Bumblebee, watch out for—!" The rest of Gears's warning was drowned out when one of Burnrate's missiles hit a freight car. Gears did not know what the freight car had contained, but it was an easy guess that the car's contents had been highly explosive. The blast was incredible, lifting the two Autobots high into the air before they tumbled and landed flat on their backs, their auditory sensors overloaded.

Gears struggled to get up. It was with only some slight satisfaction that he noticed the Decepticons had been knocked down by the blast, too. He saw Bumblebee, looking stunned and shaking his yellow-and-black head as he crawled away from the freight cars. Gears tottered to his feet. He tried to leap over the shattered freight cars and throttle Burnrate, but he tripped over the remains of a burning car and landed on his knees in the street.

Gears looked up and found Sawtooth standing above him. As Gears's sensors came back online, he heard a *click* as the spiked Decepticon loaded his missile launcher. The muzzle was three feet from Gears's head. Out of the corner of his mechanical eyes, Gears saw Bumblebee racing toward him. But he knew it was too late.

Sawtooth growled. "Good riddance, insect lover."

Gears heard a loud blast and thought that Sawtooth had fired. But then he realized that Sawtooth had stumbled slightly and was looking to his right in annoyance.

Gears followed Sawtooth's gaze and saw a police cruiser in the middle of the intersection, its blue lights flashing. The cop from the overpass was standing in front of his cruiser, the barrels of his shotgun still smoking.

"Why, you lousy little insect," Sawtooth muttered as he strode toward the police car with murderous intent.

"Sawtooth!" bellowed Blowback, still trying to stand. "Look out!"

But it was too late for Sawtooth. Bumblebee

opened fire with his plasma cannons, driving Sawtooth to his knees. Sparks flew from his perforated armor. The Decepticon fell forward on his face and skidded across the road. When his body came to a stop, the fire in his eyes was gone, replaced by a lifeless black.

Bumblebee helped Gears get up. Blowback kicked Burnrate, who scrambled up, tottering unsteadily. For a moment, the streets of Battle Mountain were silent as the four Cybertronians stared at one another.

Gears was as exhausted as he was hurt, but he wasn't about to let the Decepticons know that. As he took a step toward Blowback and Burnrate, he cycled through the weapons in his mechanical forearms, verifying that they were fully functional. Without glancing at Bumblebee, he said, "Let's get this done."

Standing beside Kevin, Douglas stared hard at the small monitor in the corridor of the Cybertronian storehouse. Douglas said, "How many items are part of your restricted inventory?"

The Cybertronian computer replied, "*One.*"

"Is the item in your restricted inventory animal, vegetable, or mineral?"

Several seconds passed before the computer answered, "*Mineral.*"

Hearing the word, Kevin felt like he'd been kicked in the stomach. If the computer were telling the truth, then Duane wasn't in the chamber behind the locked door. Duane was somewhere else. Lost.

Douglas put a hand on Kevin's shoulder. "Take it easy, Kevin. Remember, the computer is talking about inventory that's thousands of years old. Just because your brother might not be listed on the inventory doesn't mean he's not in the locked chamber."

"That's right," Kevin said hopefully. "Keep asking questions!"

Douglas took a deep breath, then said, "Is the item living or nonliving?"

"*Nonliving.*" As the computer spoke, the monitor's dim light flickered. "*My power levels are ebbing. There is a high likelihood my generators are damaged, and I may cease to function.*"

"Oh no!" Kevin cried.

Still facing the monitor, Douglas said, "If you cease to function, will the chamber open?"

"*In that event, blast doors will close, sealing off the restricted inventory. You have six questions left.*"

"Wait! That question doesn't count!"

"*Your question*," the computer said, its voice growing more sluggish, "*was related to… restricted inventory.*"

Kevin said, "I know what it is. I know what's in the chamber."

"Kevin, wait," Douglas said. "I know what you're thinking, but we need to be sure. It could be a weapon, or another computer, or something we haven't even imagined. And we don't know what will happen if we guess wrong."

"We don't have time," Kevin said. "I know what it is. I'm certain of it."

Ignoring Kevin, Douglas said, "Is the item unique, or is it a class?"

"*Multiple such items were known to exist when my inventory was established. You have five questions left.*" The light dimmed further.

Kevin said, "We don't have time for this!"

"Just give me a few more questions," Douglas said. "Is it a weapon?"

"*No.*" The computer's voice had dropped a full octave. The light went out, then came slowly back up, dimmer than before.

Douglas looked at Kevin and said, "I give up. Go ahead."

Kevin leaned closer to the grille. He said, "Is it a…a…" Although he had been thinking of a specific Cybertronian device, it was only at that moment that he realized he could only guess at the device's proper name. He crossed his fingers as he said, "Is it…a transport cylinder?"

Several seconds passed before the computer replied, "*I do not know what this term means. My power levels are dwindling.*"

Kevin looked at Douglas in horror. Trying to stay calm, Douglas said, "Computer, can your screen see an image?"

"What image?"

Douglas stabbed frantically at his phone's touch screen. Kevin peered at the screen and saw a ghostly green image of Reverb holding the Cybertronian cylinder above his head. Astonished, Kevin glared at Douglas and said, "Where did you get that picture?"

Douglas said, "Never mind that now!" He thrust his phone up to the ancient computer's barely lit screen.

"Power levels approaching zero," the computer mumbled.

"Look!" Douglas cried. "Look at this image!"

The computer's light was now barely visible. Kevin held his breath for what felt like an eternity before he heard a faint click, and then the computer said, *"Access granted."*

Kevin and Douglas hurried down the right-hand corridor. The red light had gone out, and the ancient door was slowly retracting into the floor.

The two remaining Decepticons ran in opposite directions through the town of Battle Mountain. Blowback headed toward the highway while Burnrate vaulted the freight cars and sprinted toward the river. Gears stomped after Blowback. Bumblebee took off in pursuit of Burnrate.

Bumblebee chased Burnrate through a small park and then down a quiet street past houses and trees. The fleeing Decepticon snagged a power line, snapping it in his haste to escape as Bumblebee advanced. Bumblebee sorted through his vast library of pop songs before his audio speaker blasted, *"Nowhere to run to, baby…"*

Reaching a wide, unpaved area on the edge of town, Burnrate turned and shot a huge fireball at Bumblebee. Bumblebee ignored the threat and kept running, leaping through the flames despite a scream of protest from his temperature sensors. He caught Burnrate by the throat and hurled him over a fence into a dusty lot.

Burnrate hit the ground and tumbled to a stop. He was still struggling to get up when Bumblebee tackled him, wrapping his arms around the Decepticon's neck. Burnrate staggered across the lot, writhing and kicking in an effort to break Bumblebee's hold. As Bumblebee held tightly, he noticed a structure to his left and a sign that read BATTLE MOUNTAIN RODEO GROUNDS. Inspired by the sign, Bumblebee began playing the theme music to his favorite Western movie.

Burnrate finally fell, but as he hit the ground,

he gnashed his metal teeth and tried to bring his weapon-laden arm toward Bumblebee. Bumblebee's only option was to defend himself. He slammed his knee down on Burnrate's arm as he fired his pulse cannon at the Decepticon's chest.

Bumblebee stood up. Burnrate wasn't moving and would never move again. As Bumblebee swaggered out of the rodeo grounds and past the wreckage of Battle Mountain's streets, he continued playing the Western music. He wondered what he would look like if he wore a cowboy hat.

Gears ran after Blowback as fast as his damaged leg would allow, passing ranch houses and trailers and ducking the desperate volleys of fire the Decepticon flung back over his shoulder. Seeing the highway ahead, Gears stopped, took careful aim at Blowback with his missile launcher, and then fired.

The missile streaked toward Blowback and struck near his feet, blasting him up into the air. He landed hard, his head and shoulders driving into the dirt before he rolled to a stop. Blowback shook his head groggily, then rose and stumbled off the main road, smashing through a gas station and a chain-link fence.

Gears saw Blowback fall and vanish from sight. He chugged ahead, stepped over the broken chain-link fence, and saw that Blowback had fallen into a swimming pool. The pool's once-blue water was now cloudy with oily lubricant.

Blowback thrashed in the pool and activated his ax, sending a churning cone of water into Gears's face. When Gears's vision cleared, he saw that Blowback had jumped out of the pool and was now limping across a green field. Y-shaped metal posts rose above two ends of the field, and on the posts, large letters spelled out LONGHORNS.

Gears realized they had arrived at a football field. He recognized the layout because Iron-hide liked to study that particular sport, claim-ing it offered insight into humans' strategic thinking. Gears had watched a few televised football games with Ironhide. Based on how and when Ironhide would shout enthusiastically during the games, Gears suspected Ironhide also liked the violence.

Blowback stopped on the field's fifty-yard line and turned to face Gears. The Decepticon's ax became a blur at the end of his arm. Gears eyed the spinning ax blade warily as he took several steps backward, moving to the nearest metal goalpost. He yanked it out of the ground and broke it, leaving himself holding a long yellow pole.

Blowback roared and charged. Gears swung the goalpost at his opponent. Unfortunately, Gears didn't have a firm grip on the goalpost, and when it hit the spinning ax blades, it was knocked aside by their momentum, flying out of Gears's hand and leaving him unprotected. He felt a blast of air from the spinning blades a split second before the blades bit deeply into his left shoulder, driving him to his knees as Blowback rolled across the ground and came up fast, poised for his next attack.

That didn't go as planned, Gears thought. He tried to lift his left arm but found it inoperative, and it dangled uselessly at his side. Gears's feedback sensors screamed in mechanical agony. He turned them off. They weren't telling him anything he didn't already know.

Blowback charged again, his ax blades whipping in a deadly, screaming circle. Gears was still on his knees, and he saw the fallen goalpost on the grass beside him. He extended his still-functional right arm to grab the goalpost. He dragged it in front of him, lifting it and bracing it against the ground as Blowback closed the distance between them.

Blowback swung his ax, but Gears rapidly angled the goalpost to take the impact. The ax blades bit into the goalpost, but Gears held on as tightly as he could, using his right leg as a brace against the lower half of the goalpost to keep it anchored in the ground. A shriek of stressed metal filled the air as Blowback's ax blades tore free of their moorings. The blades flew thirty feet across the field before they bit into the ground. Blowback screamed furiously, then tripped over the goalpost and fell on his face in the grass.

Gears flung himself on the fallen Decepticon. Blowback grabbed at Gears's left arm and laughed as he tried to pull the arm out of its socket, but Gears wrapped his right arm around Blowback's metal neck and wrenched it as hard as he could. Gears heard an ugly snap of metal, and then Blowback went limp.

Touchdown, Gears thought grimly, tossing the Decepticon into the end zone. He trudged off the field, heading back to where he had last seen Bumblebee.

Kevin and Douglas found a single object inside the unlocked chamber within the Cybertronian storehouse. The object was a cylinder that appeared to be identical to the one discovered at the Hawthorne Army Depot. Clearly fascinated by the cylinder, Douglas walked around it as he recorded data with his sophisticated cell phone.

Kevin saw four small, glassy rectangles on one side of the cylinder. Unlike the melted rectangles on the pillar that Chief Lindsay had been examining at the NEST base, the rectangles on the present pillar looked undamaged. Kevin suspected the tube was still operational, but he didn't know how it worked.

Kevin noticed Douglas leaning closer to the cylinder. "Don't touch it!" Kevin said. "I want to try talking with the computer again." He ran out of the chamber and returned to the monitor and grille at the intersection of corridors. The computer's screen was flickering.

"Computer! Are you still there?"

The computer's voice was soft, garbled, and agonizingly slow as it responded, *"Power... levels... minimal."*

"The cylinder in the chamber... What *is* it? Any information you have about it, you need to tell me!"

Silence. Frustrated, Kevin struck the wall with the side of his fist. He feared the computer might never speak again, but then it mumbled, *"Prototype... trans-spatial... technology."*

"How does it *work*?"

"It... does... not... work.... Catastrophic mal... malfunctions... Production... dis... discontinued."

"Okay, but if it *did* work, how would you operate it?"

"I... was... not made... to operate... it."

"Then what about me?!" Kevin said desperately.

"Or a Cybertronian! Or anybody! How would someone operate it? How?!"

"*Set…numerical…coordinates. Auto… auto…automatic…timer.*" And then the screen went black, and the light winked out.

Kevin shouted, "Douglas!"

"I'm here," Douglas replied as he emerged from the darkness, moving back up the corridor to rejoin Kevin. Douglas had his phone up to his ear and was speaking quietly into it. He led Kevin back to the entrance, and they stepped out onto the rocky shelf.

As frustrated by their situation as Kevin was, he was relieved to breathe fresh air again. Looking down at the town of Battle Mountain, he saw a few small fires were burning, and he heard the wail of fire engines. "Where are Gears and Bumblebee? Is the fight over?"

Douglas ignored Kevin as he said into his

phone, "Good. Do so immediately." He put his phone back in his pocket.

Kevin said, "Who were you talking to?"

"The Hyperdynamix warehouse outside Winnemucca. I ordered them to send a truck for the cylinder."

"What?" Kevin was outraged. "You can't do that! I don't care if you and your father are rich! You can't take the device to Hyperdynamix. It has to go to the NEST base!"

Douglas glared at Kevin. "That's exactly what I just told the warehouse manager. The truck will deliver the artifact to the NEST base."

Surprised and embarrassed, Kevin said, "Oh."

"I've risked my life out here, Kevin. For you, and for your brother, and for the Autobots. All while having no idea if my own father is still alive. But after everything I've done to help, you still don't trust me?"

"I'm sorry," Kevin said. "I'm really sorry. I just thought…I thought you were going to take the cylinder and that I'd lose my only chance of finding my brother. I'm worried about him. That's all."

Douglas tilted his head back and looked up at the stars. Then he lowered his gaze, nodded, and stuck out his hand. The two boys solemnly shook hands. Then Douglas looked at the town below and said, "Look there! It's Bumblebee and Gears!"

Chapter Fifteen
ESCAPE VELOCITY

Looking down from the rock shelf outside the Cybertronian storehouse, Kevin spotted Gears and Bumblebee. From hundreds of feet away, Kevin could tell Gears was hurt. His left arm dangled by his side, and his limp looked worse. Bumblebee appeared to be scouting the area ahead of them, but then he trotted back to check on his fellow Autobot.

Kevin and Douglas saw the two Autobots come to a halt where they'd left the boys. Gears and Bumblebee looked around, apparently searching for them. The stars were still out in the west, but the eastern sky was streaked with the first light of dawn. Kevin began leaping up and down and yelling the Autobots' names, trying to get their attention.

At last, the Autobots turned their heads, and they stared up into the hills. Seeing Kevin and Douglas, they began the laborious climb up the slopes. Despite Gears's injuries, he still moved with surprising speed. Minutes later, Gears and Bumblebee arrived outside the entrance to the Cybertronian storehouse.

Gears looked at the open entrance for a moment before he turned his gaze to Kevin and Douglas. Kevin was certain he saw disapproval in his friend's bright blue eyes. Bumblebee placed his hands on his hips as he shook his head at the boys.

Gears said, "It was extremely unwise to enter the storehouse without us. You could have been killed."

"We're fine," Kevin said. "But are *you* all right?"

"I am repairable," Gears said. "Did you find any sign of your brother?"

"I'm afraid not," Kevin said. "But we're pretty sure we found a working transport cylinder."

Douglas said, "A Hyperdynamix truck will be here in a few minutes and will take the cylinder back to the NEST base. If you can move it down to the road, our work here is done."

Kevin said, "Are you sure it's safe to move the thing? What if it activates?"

"It shouldn't," Gears said. "Reverb did something to operate it. As long as we handle it carefully and don't touch any moving parts, I believe we can move it safely."

Douglas's cell phone buzzed. He peered at its screen, then said, "The truck will be here in a few minutes."

"Really?" Kevin said. "I didn't think it could get here so soon."

Only seconds later, they caught sight of the truck, a long white shape in the gloom. Douglas said something softly into his phone. Gears looked at Bumblebee and said, "Let's move the cylinder down to the road."

"Wait!" said Kevin. He pointed to headlights approaching from the south. "Someone else is coming. And really fast, too."

Douglas said, "It's just a car."

Kevin said, "If I've learned anything over the past month, it's to never assume a car is just a car."

"Good point," Douglas admitted. A moment

later, the car slowed to a halt about a mile away, and the headlights switched off.

"Where'd the car go?" Kevin said. "Gears, can you see anything?"

Gears switched his visual sensors over to telescopic mode and stared into the gloom. Then he went rigid. "It's Reverb."

"What?" Kevin gasped. "That's impossible!"

"I am 98.795 percent certain that it is Reverb."

Kevin turned quickly to face Douglas and said, "Tell your driver to get out of sight!"

Douglas frowned as he tapped away at his cell phone. He said, "If it is Reverb, I suspect he's coming for the storehouse, not for the truck."

Gears said, "Bumblebee, we should leave here to fight Reverb below, so that Kevin and Douglas can get to safety."

Kevin heard the weariness in Gears's voice. Gears tried to lift his left arm, but it made a pained grinding noise. Kevin said, "You can't fight him, Gears. You're hurt."

"I will do my best," Gears said. He could see Reverb striding down the center line of the highway below them. "Come on, Bumblebee."

"No!" Kevin yelled as the Autobots started down the slope. "Gears, you can't!"

Gears and Bumblebee had only descended a few steps when Kevin heard the distant whir of rotors. A military helicopter emerged from over the mountains, flying low and fast toward them. Seconds later, Kevin was able to identify the aircraft as a NEST transport helicopter. The copter's wide bay doors were open. Standing inside the bay was Ironhide.

Gears and Bumblebee stopped and looked at

the copter. Ironhide leaped down and landed on the rocky shelf beside Kevin and Douglas. The scarred old Autobot growled. "Looks like we've got some Autobots gone AWOL. Not to mention a couple of kids up way past their bedtimes."

Kevin was so thrilled to see Ironhide that he didn't care that the weapons specialist was obviously angry. Gesturing to the storehouse's entrance, he said, "We found a transport cylinder inside, Ironhide. Nothing else. But you have to help Gears and Bumblebee. Reverb escaped, and he's down there!"

Ironhide chuckled. "Nice of Reverb to run straight to where I can get my mitts on him." Looking down at Bumblebee and Gears, he pointed to the hovering copter and said, "Want a ride down?"

But before Gears or Bumblebee could respond, Ironhide surveyed the land below and said, "Aw, nuts." The others followed his gaze to see that Reverb had changed into a black jeep and was headed at top speed for the town of Battle Mountain. Watching Reverb race off, Ironhide muttered, "What a chicken."

Gears said, "Are we not going to pursue?"

"That's a negative," Ironhide said. "First thing we have to do is secure the contents of this storehouse, which fortunately seems to be just one pillar. Then we have to head at top speed to Hyperdynamix, so we can help Optimus, Ratchet, some NEST commandos, and this young pup's father." He gestured to Douglas.

"Pup?" Douglas said.

"That's right, puppy," Ironhide said as he

watched Reverb vanish to the north. "Tough luck. I've been itching for another round with Reverb."

"You can still catch him!" Douglas said urgently. "There's a Hyperdynamix truck down below. The driver came at my orders. The truck can take the pillar to the NEST base while you go after Reverb!"

"No," Ironhide said as he looked at Gears and Bumblebee.

Douglas said, "What do you mean, no?"

Ironhide turned in disbelief, then stepped toward Douglas, forcing the boy to back up against the rock face. Ironhide bent down so his massive, pitted metal head was inches from Douglas's face. "What I mean," Ironhide said, "is N-O. As in N-O, I take my orders from Optimus Prime, and his orders were very clear. As for you, kid, you can give all the orders you like to truck drivers and toy tanks, but you better not ever even *dream* of trying to tell me what to do again. You got that?"

Douglas nodded slowly. He looked slightly scared, but mostly he looked angry. Kevin wanted to support Douglas, to tell Ironhide everything Douglas had done to help that night. But one look at Ironhide's grim face convinced him that it would be a very bad idea for him to say anything at the moment.

It didn't take long for Ironhide, Bumblebee, and Gears to remove the cylinder from the storehouse's chamber and pack it up. As they worked, Gears told Ironhide about the events that had led to the fight with the four Decepticons at Battle Mountain. After the Autobots loaded the cylinder into the NEST copter, they piled in, taking the boys with them. As the copter lifted away, Kevin looked at Ironhide and said, "I'm sorry if I disappointed you."

"*You're* sorry?" Ironhide said as he adjusted his built-in radio. "I hate to think what Optimus Prime will say to me after I report!"

Chapter Sixteen
ENDGAME

At the Hyperdynamix compound, the rumbling boom of an explosion alerted Optimus Prime and General Marcus to the fact that their situation was about to get a lot more dangerous. A moment after the explosion, Marcus received a call from Alexander Porter, who was still in the compound's control room. Porter yelled, "The Decepticons are on the move, General! We see them on our security cameras! Main Level

Corridor A, Sub-Level Corridor F, Sub-Level Corridor C!"

Several blasts rattled the buildings throughout the Hyperdynamix complex. Outside the main building, an array of NEST commandos nervously eyed the entrance's broad doors.

General Marcus cupped one hand over his headset and said, "Which way are the Decepticons heading, Doctor?"

"Your way, but...they're destroying everything in their path! Fuel cells, labs...They're wrecking it all!"

Optimus Prime took a heavy step away from Marcus as he activated his own built-in communicator. "Ratchet, move to cover the exit from Sub-Level Corridor C."

"Roger that," Ratchet replied. "What took them so long to move?"

"We can only guess," Optimus said.

General Marcus looked at Optimus and said, "I'm sending Carbon-Fiber Teams A and B into the other two corridors to try to drive the Decepticons toward us. I just wish a few more of your Autobots were here."

"So do I," Optimus said.

The radios had been quiet throughout the long night while the invading Decepticons had remained concealed within the complex. Now, the radios buzzed with nervous chatter, status updates, and requests for orders. Optimus heard Ratchet say, "Engaging," and the rapid-fire rattle of pulse cannons followed the single word. Then Optimus heard the whine of a saw and the shriek of rending metal. Next came a grunt of exertion and a huge crash.

Optimus said, "Ratchet?"

"One down," Ratchet replied, the shriek of

his saw diminishing to a whine. "Moving to assist the NEST teams in F. Tell them I'm coming. I do not wish to be encased in carbon-fiber."

"Roger that," General Marcus said before he passed along the advisory. He glanced up at the towering form of Optimus. "Your medical officer makes for a very effective soldier."

"Much to his regret," Optimus said. "He would much rather heal than harm."

The radio buzzed again. "Carbon-Fiber Team A. We are engaging!" Fire stuttered over the speakers, along with the *whoosh* of the NEST cannons, spraying rapidly solidifying carbon-fiber at the Decepticons. A soldier yelled, "Heading your way, boss!"

"This is Dr. Porter...Movement in Main Corridor A!"

Optimus Prime glanced down at General

Marcus. "You and your men should get behind me," he said calmly as his great glowing Energon blade extended from his forearm. Optimus was about to step forward when he heard another sound. He looked up and saw a NEST copter descending. "Reinforcements," he said. "Just in time."

The main doors to the Hyperdynamix compound exploded outward. Two dark-armored Decepticons raced out of the thick black smoke that billowed from the entranceway, firing their pulse cannons wildly. The NEST commandos ducked and fired back, filling the courtyard with deafening reports of gunfire.

As Optimus moved quickly to cut off the fleeing Decepticons, he caught sight of a yellow shape striding through the smoke behind them. Optimus bellowed, "Hold your fire!" just as the first Decepticon smashed into him. The

Autobot leader took the blow and countered it with his great sword. The Decepticon parried desperately with his own metal arm, but Optimus grabbed the arm and gave it a hard twist, bending it sharply. The Decepticon howled as he tried to shove his pulse cannon against Optimus's side.

Optimus kicked the Decepticon, sending him tumbling across the concrete. A missile whistled past his hip as the other Decepticon tried to escape. The fleeing Decepticon's right leg was encrusted with gray threads of carbon-fiber, which had formed into a rope trailing behind him.

Distracted, Optimus took his eye off the first Decepticon for a moment, long enough for the Decepticon to unfold a gleaming spike from his undamaged forearm. Optimus caught the arm before the blow could land, shoved away the

Decepticon, then swung his Energon blade and took him out.

The other Decepticon had made it past Optimus and the NEST commandos, but he came to a skidding stop as the black NEST copter landed in front of him. Ironhide and Bumblebee jumped out, followed by a slower-moving Gears.

Ironhide lifted his arms like a muscleman posing on a beach, then re-formed both arms into massive cannons as he roared, "Game over!" But before Ironhide could fire, Ratchet grabbed the strand of carbon-fiber trailing behind the escaping Decepticon and pulled hard, dragging the living robot backward.

"Boss!" yelled Ratchet, and Optimus swung his blade again, defeating the last intruder.

"Aw, nuts!" Ironhide said. "No fair! No way! He was *mine*! I *had* him!"

While Ironhide raged, Kevin and Douglas climbed down from the copter, its rotors still spinning lazily. Optimus Prime retracted his blade as he walked toward Bumblebee, Gears, and the two boys. General Marcus followed and stood before the boys. "You two have a lot of explaining to do," he said.

"Excuse me, General," Optimus said. He looked down at Kevin before he let his gaze travel over the others. "Ironhide briefed me on what happened at Battle Mountain, and I am relieved to see all of you are safe. But I am also enormously disappointed that you could be so irresponsible. You went off on your own, without authorization, leaving a key NEST facility largely unprotected, a situation that contributed to the escape of one of our most dangerous enemies."

Optimus pointed at the two wrecked Cybertronians. "The Decepticons are a rabble, ruled

by their emotions," he continued. "It is one reason we have so far prevailed in this war, despite
being badly outnumbered. But if we are undis-
ciplined, if we ignore orders, we risk that advantage. Which means that we risk *everything*. Do
you understand that?"

Gears nodded, then elbowed Bumblebee, who
was looking at the ground and wishing he were
anywhere else. Bumblebee nodded, too. Kevin
tried to will his knees to stop knocking as he
stepped forward and said, "Optimus Prime...
sir?"

"Kevin Bowman," Optimus rumbled. "Tell
me you at least did your homework."

"No...I didn't," Kevin said. "But I just wanted
to say that I'm really sorry. I was so scared for
my brother that I got it into my head that he
had to be there, inside the storehouse at Battle

Mountain. I thought if I didn't rescue him, I'd never see him again."

Optimus said softly, "But he wasn't there, was he, Kevin?"

"No, sir," Kevin said miserably.

"So you risked your life on a false hope. As well as the lives of your friends. This is what I mean by responsibility."

"Optimus," Douglas said, "don't be too hard on Kevin. It was really my fault. I was the one who asked Kevin for help. And I was the one who encouraged him and Gears and Bumblebee to leave the base."

"It is admirable that you would admit this," Optimus said. "But I do not understand something. According to Ironhide's report, you knew of the danger posed by Blowback at Battle Mountain, yet instead of informing General

Marcus or me, you put yourself in great danger. Why didn't you tell us?"

"Because I was afraid for my father," Douglas said. "I thought if you knew about Blowback, you would decide you had to defend the storehouse and you would leave my father here to die."

Optimus nodded. "War brings hard choices, Douglas Porter," he said. "But we will never leave anyone to die."

The sound of footsteps came from the courtyard behind them. General Marcus turned and said, "Ah! Speaking of Dr. Porter, here he comes now."

Alexander Porter's long gray hair was wild, and his eyes were red with lack of sleep. He glared at Optimus Prime before he spied General Marcus, then he snapped, "Look at my complex! Do you know how much damage has been done to my property and business? Do you grasp the enormity of the setbacks to our research?"

"The damage is regrettable," Optimus said evenly. "But by showing restraint, I believe we saved many lives. And you and your son are safe."

Surprised, Porter peered around Optimus and caught sight of Douglas.

"Hello, Father," Douglas spoke up. "I'm glad you're all right."

"No thanks to you or your allies," Porter said. "Just look at this damage! It's terrible. My life's work!"

Kevin saw Douglas's face harden and grow cold. "Yes, Father," Douglas said. "It's truly heartbreaking."

Optimus turned to regard the cylinder lashed to the deck of the transport copter. He said,

"Autobots, we are returning to the NEST base. Chief Lindsay will want to investigate this second artifact immediately."

"Best news I've heard all night," Ironhide growled as the Autobots clambered aboard. "I'm tuckered out."

Optimus's blue eyes narrowed. "I don't see why *you* should be tired, Ironhide. While the rest of us were fighting Decepticons, all you did was fly around Nevada."

"What?! *Boss!* First, I had to fly back to NEST, and then..."

Bumblebee began to snicker, followed by the rest of the Autobots. Ironhide's furious complaints trailed off and then he glowered at Optimus.

Ironhide grumbled to himself as he stalked off. "Everyone's a comedian."

Chief Lindsay was indeed eager to examine the second Cybertronian cylinder. And after hearing Kevin's account of his conversation with the ancient computer, and then examining notes from the Witwicky incident, Lindsay was able to verify that the ancient device was operational.

"Look here," he told Kevin. "These four rectangles are dials that set the numerical values, and this switch here—no, I'm not going to press it—begins the countdown. Judging from the power levels, the cylinder will only operate once. Despite its age, I'm certain it will work."

Kevin studied the dials and said, "But how do we know what numerical value to set?"

Lindsay frowned. "We don't. Cybertronian

mathematics uses a base-ten positional nota-
tion just like we do, so there'd be thousands of
possibilities."

"You're saying there are a thousand places
where my brother could have been transported,"
Kevin said. "But we don't know which one.
And the pillar will only work once."

"That's right," Lindsay said, pleased that
Kevin was following the discussion. Then he
saw the horror on the boy's face and added,
"I'm sorry, Kevin, but...that's right."

Alexander Porter was still ranting about the
damage to the Hyperdynamix compound hours
after the Porters' private helicopter brought him
and his son back to their sprawling mountain-
top home. Standing before a picture window in

their living room, Porter said, "You know the strangest thing, Douglas? The twelve prototype tanks were stolen, but there was no sign of intrusion in that part of the complex. And the security logs have been erased. Not just from after the Decepticon attack, but for the whole day. Yet there were no other attempts to break into our system."

"What's strange about that?" Douglas asked. "We know the Decepticons can infiltrate computer systems. Our security's good, but it can't stop hackers from other planets."

Porter rubbed his chin thoughtfully. "I'm not convinced the theft and the raid are related. I believe it's possible that the tanks were stolen before the Decepticons even got there."

"That doesn't make any sense," Douglas said. "I mean, the Decepticons must have been involved in the theft somehow, or else they wouldn't have been at the complex, right? And if the goal was to steal our tanks, why would the Decepticons stick around inside the complex to get slaughtered?"

"I don't know," his father admitted as he turned to stare out the window. "It's all very strange."

"I'm sure it will be clear in time," Douglas said. "Now excuse me, Father. I've got...homework to do...."

Alexander Porter nodded absentmindedly as he continued staring out the window. He didn't see the venomous look his son aimed at his back before leaving the living room.

This job is getting worse all the time, Simon Clay thought.

It had been scary enough arranging the infiltration of Hyperdynamix, hacking into their systems to plant phony orders that gave his trucks access to the loading dock, then erasing those orders, shutting down security cameras, and wiping security logs.

But at least he'd been able to do that without a giant robot standing behind him all the time. Ever since Clay had used the tiny robot to break Reverb out of the NEST base, Reverb had been a walking hulk of pure menace, from the scowl on his metal face to the deadly looking cannon sticking out of his chest. Clay tried to avoid direct eye contact with Reverb as the phone rang, and Clay saw the caller was Stealth Leader.

"Go ahead, boss," Clay said, trying to sound authoritative, like he was on top of the situation.

"Put me on speaker," said the distorted, electronically modulated voice. "Is Reverb there?"

"I am here," Reverb replied. "Though I dislike sharing quarters with this insect."

Stealth Leader said, "Would you prefer it back in your cell at NEST? Because I can arrange that just as easily."

Reverb muttered, "My accommodations are sufficient."

"Good," Stealth Leader said. "Now, to business. The Hyperdynamix raid was nearly a disaster. The Decepticons were supposed to cover their tracks, with the damage making it look like the tanks were stolen during the attack. Instead they didn't even touch the room. Alexander Porter is suspicious."

"They had their orders!" Clay protested. "I did my best, but the Decepticons wouldn't listen! And then they got themselves blasted, running like frightened rabbits right into the Autobots!"

"That doesn't matter," Stealth Leader said. "Neither does the loss of the four Decepticons at Battle Mountain. Pawns, all of them."

Reverb growled. "Is that what you consider *me*? A pawn?!"

"Hardly," Stealth Leader said. "You're one of the most important pieces on the game board. When we're finished with this conversation, Clay will show you our new prototype tanks. How'd you like to lead your own army, Reverb?"

"Who wouldn't?" Reverb said gleefully.

"Glad to hear it," Stealth Leader said. "We'll have work to do, recovering from the mess at Hyperdynamix. But my plans are advancing.

And soon, very soon, the Autobots will fall. Stealth Leader out."

Douglas shut down the laptop, leaned back in his black office chair, and considered all that had happened in the last twenty-four hours.

Clay had botched the raid on Hyperdynamix. The interfering Ironhide had foiled his attempt to snatch the transport cylinder away for his own uses. And Reverb and Blowback hadn't eliminated any of the Autobots.

But all in all, Douglas thought, *things had gone well.*

He had displayed his usual gift for social engineering, for making people do what he wanted without ever suspecting it. His father had played his role perfectly by acting like an ungrateful child in front of the Autobots, which helped set up Douglas's next move. And as for the Autobots' little pet Kevin Bowman, he now trusted Douglas completely.

Manipulating Kevin was so easy, Douglas thought. With minimal effort, Douglas had tricked Kevin and his Autobot allies into the trip to Battle Mountain, and to open up the ancient storehouse. Now, it seemed all of the Autobots trusted him. *Except perhaps for Ironhide.* But Douglas believed he could somehow make Ironhide's reservations work to his own advantage.

The more Douglas thought about recent events, he decided his biggest regret was the loss of the Cybertronian cylinder.

He activated his laptop and navigated through his files until he found a video of Reverb throwing the first cylinder at the soldiers at Hawthorne.

However, the video was not from the same file that he'd shown Kevin. That version had been missing a few crucial seconds at the beginning.

Douglas hit pause and zoomed in. His hackers had done an excellent job enhancing the image quality. Douglas could clearly read the Cybertronian numbers on the cylinder's readout, the numbers that indicated where the ancient machine would transport any captured material or life-forms.

Douglas took a screen grab of the image and moved it to a secured folder on his computer. He knew Kevin Bowman would do anything to get a look at that particular picture. And if Kevin played his role properly, Douglas allowed the possibility that he might just let Kevin see it.

Epilogue

Sergeant Duane Bowman and his fellow soldiers didn't know the name of the world they were marooned on, but they called it Blue Planet, named after the light from the world's sun.

It was colder than on Earth, or maybe it was just winter. And the air smelled different, like something just out of sight had gone rotten. But at least the men could breathe in the atmosphere. Duane knew that was good luck, all things considered.

He had tried to stop thinking of his last moments on Earth, of the alien robot flinging that strange rod in front of his squad mates... the agony of feeling his body bend like taffy as he and the others were pulled through some kind of vortex that had spat them out on Blue Planet, with no way to get back.

Duane shook his head. He couldn't think that way. None of the men could. If they did, they might as well give up, lie down, and die here, unimaginably far from home.

They weren't going to do that. Duane wouldn't *let* them do that.

"Listen up!" he barked at the other four soldiers. "It'll be night soon, and those wolf things will be back. We need to get a fire built and set up watches. Remember, we don't have a lot of ammo, so don't waste it. Fire short, controlled bursts, and only when you know you have a target. Let's not jump at shadows."

His squad mates nodded. They looked grim but determined.

"We can do this," Duane insisted, looking each soldier in the eye. "We will rely on one another. We will help one another. We will survive. And we will get home. I don't know how, but I promise you . . . we *will* get home."

TO BE CONTINUED . . .